A FATAL ASSIGNATION

PREVIOUS NOVELS BY ALICE CHETWYND LEY:

A Reputation Dies
The Intrepid Miss Haydon
A Conformable Wife
A Regency Scandal
An Advantageous Marriage
At the Dark of the Moon
The Beau and the Bluestocking
Beloved Diana
The Sentimental Spy
The Master and the Maiden
Toast of the Town
A Season at Brighton
The Courting of Joanna
The Clandestine Betrothal
The Georgian Rake
The Jewelled Snuff Box

A FATAL ASSIGNATION

A Novel by

ALICE CHETWYND LEY

St. Martin's Press
New York

DEDICATION

In memory of my father, F.G. Humphrey, O.B.E. and of the story sessions we all enjoyed on family holidays long ago.

Library of Congress Cataloging-in-Publication Data

Ley, Alice Chetwynd.
A fatal assignation.

I. Title.
PR6062.E965F3 1987 823'.914 87-4446
ISBN 0-312-00596-2

First published in Great Britain by Severn House Publishers Ltd.

First U.S. Edition

10 9 8 7 6 5 4 3 2 1

A FATAL ASSIGNATION

CHAPTER I

Curiosity was an integral part of Miss Anthea Rutherford's character. She could no more resist exploring an intriguing situation than a bee could be restrained from gathering nectar. It was because of this regrettable tendency that she first became involved in a mystery concerning a well-known gentleman of the *ton*, who was also an intimate friend of no less a personage than the Prince Regent.

It all seemed quite simple at the time. Miss Rutherford was keeping an appointment for a dress fitting at Madame Yvonne's modish salon in Bond Street. All the *ton* ladies patronised Madame Yvonne, said to be a French émigrée, possibly of aristocratic blood, who had reached these shores some twenty or so years ago with little besides an undoubted French flair for dress and a determination to make a prosperous living for herself. Her present establishment and exclusive clientele bore witness to the success of her efforts.

Anthea alighted from the family town coach with instructions to the coachman to return for her presently. She airily waved aside her maid, who had been about to accompany her into the shop.

'No, Martha, stroll about a little instead, if you wish. It will amuse you more than sitting indoors waiting for me.'

Martha, a sensible looking woman close on forty years

of age, looked grateful for the reprieve.

As Anthea entered the elegant green and gold showroom of Madame Yvonne's premises, she was greeted briefly by the proprietress. The Honourable Anthea Rutherford, youngest daughter of Viscount Rutherford, was a valued client and as such could usually count upon claiming Madame's undivided attention. Unfortunately, today it was already being claimed by an equally important older lady who was in the process of placing a large order with the firm. Madame was therefore obliged to hand Miss Rutherford into the care of a minion before returning to her previous customer, whom she proceeded to lead out of the salon and into the adjoining workroom to inspect various samples of dress materials.

Usually the faithful Miss Parker was at hand to deal with exigencies of this kind, but there was no sign of her now. Instead, a young assistant, ill at ease and uncertain, hastened to obey Madame's parting instruction to show Miss Rutherford into a fitting room and summon the dressmaker responsible for her new gown. She hesitated for a moment before guiding her client to a small closet on the extreme right of the showroom and on the opposite side from the fitting rooms Anthea had used on previous occasions. Here the attendant left her with many incoherent apologies, though for what offence Anthea could not imagine.

As she looked about her, however, it began to appear that the girl had conducted her to a room much inferior to any she had previously occupied. There was no chair, for one thing; and instead of several full length pier glasses disposed about the room, there was only a small square mirror on one wall. It was even a trifle spotted with age.

For a few moments, Anthea amused herself in gazing at her reflection with laughing dark eyes and deciding that the pink bonnet she was wearing was really quite becoming. Then she turned to look about her once more before returning to the salon, as obviously a mistake had been made, and it would be better to give the poor girl time to correct it before her employer appeared on the scene.

She forgot all that in a moment, however, when her quick eyes discovered the outline of a cleverly concealed door on the left hand wall. It was masked by the stripes of the green and gold wallpaper and with its handle lying flat against a strip of oak timbering running around the walls at chest height.

A secret door leading to exciting places?

Well, most likely not, she thought regretfully, after the first surge of excitement. It probably opened into nothing more mysterious than a cupboard.

All the same, she could not resist the challenge. She grasped the handle and turned it.

The door opened inwards, revealing a small enclosed space in front of yet another, more solid door.

She hesitated, feeling a momentary pang of guilt at venturing to intrude on someone's privacy. But curiosity proved too strong for her; she took a step forward and quietly opened the second door a few inches, peering round it.

The room beyond was luxuriously appointed with a thick red carpet on the floor, red and white striped satin covers to the mahogany furniture and discreet lighting. At first she thought it was empty. Then she noticed a gentleman seated upon the elegant sofa to her right. She had a full view of his face, but his expression gave no indication of his having noticed the partly opened door or the intruder looking through it.

She recognised the gentleman at once. He was a well known member of the *ton* and one of the Prince Regent's circle. He was also of her father's generation, but certainly not a personal friend. Prinney numbered several gentlemen among his acquaintance whom Viscount Rutherford would unhesitatingly describe as 'loose fish'. Anthea, who was surprisingly well informed in scandalous slang for a gently nurtured young lady of nineteen, understood this to mean that Sir Aubrey Jermyn was a womaniser.

He must on no account catch sight of her, she thought in sudden panic, for he could not fail to recognise her, as she was a friend of his niece and ward, Charlotte.

Quickly but quietly she closed the door and returned to her tiny closet to shut herself in just as the assistant returned with the dressmaker.

There followed an icy reprimand for the unfortunate girl, abject apologies to Anthea and a swift removal to a larger, more opulent fitting room. Thereafter, her business was concluded in the usual efficient manner, with Madame Yvonne, now at liberty, personally conducting her to her carriage.

A fashionably dressed lady, known to Anthea as one of London's foremost hostesses and married into a family of great antiquity and prestige, was alighting from a carriage outside the premises just as Anthea stepped into hers. Anthea and the lady exchanged bows, while Madame Yvonne at once took the newcomer under her wing, escorting her into the salon.

Anthea's finely etched brows drew together for a few moments as she pondered the mystery of Sir Aubrey Jermyn's presence in Madame Yvonne's private apartments. There was no likelihood of an amorous liaison there; business was the ruling passion of the elderly Frenchwoman's life, as everyone knew. Neither would any gentleman have been shown into the private part of the house had he escorted some lady to the modiste's. On such very rare occasions, the unfortunate male would find himself accommodated in the salon itself on one of those highly decorative but excruciatingly uncomfortable small chairs of gilded wood with striped green and gold satin covers. Anthea had seen this occur only once in the several years of her own and her mama's association with the establishment; she recalled feeling extremely sorry for the victim, who had looked, and doubtless felt, as out of place as any man would do in such surroundings. Most took care to avoid the ordeal.

But if Sir Aubrey were not there for either of these reasons, then why? He had looked as if he were awaiting someone . . .

She shrugged, dismissing the matter from her mind with a rueful smile. It would be for some stupid reason, not in the least bit exciting, just like the door which she had hoped might lead to some unusual place, the threshold of an adventure. But now she came to consider, there were often such concealed doors leading out of drawing rooms into a narrow landing and the servants' staircase. She remembered there had been one at Wimpole Hall, where she had visited recently with her parents.

She sighed. Really, life was not nearly so exciting as one always hoped it would be. Of course, there had been rare fun a few months ago, when she had been able to give her Uncle Justin some trifling assistance in the matter of investigating a murder.* But one could scarcely hope for anything of that kind to chance in one's way again.

Sir Aubrey Jermyn and his wife Amelia had been married for close on twenty years and led admirably self-contained lives. When at his town house, Jermyn spent most of his time at his clubs or with the Carlton House set; when he was at his country estate in Sussex, he occupied himself in the usual male sporting activities. Lady Jermyn passed her days in the approved manner for a lady of Quality;

* *Vide* 'A Reputation Dies'.

paying social calls, shopping in the fashionable quarter, and chaperoning her husband's nineteen-year-old niece and ward, Charlotte. Husband and wife appeared together at social gatherings whenever custom or the particular invitation required this, but otherwise their ways lay apart. It was a marriage in the accepted mode.

Nevertheless, Lady Jermyn always knew where her husband might be found should he decide to absent himself for a few days. Such occasions were usually mentioned in advance, so as not to interfere with their joint engagements. And she had never known him to stay anywhere overnight without taking his valet.

This was why it came as a surprise to her to discover on this particular morning that not only had her husband failed to sleep at home on the preceding night, but that Preston, his man, was still in the house.

She summoned Preston and questioned him, careful to make her voice sound casual.

'I wonder, did Sir Aubrey chance to mention to you that he wouldn't be returning home yesterday evening? He may have said something about it to me, but I have forgot – I fear I've the wretchedest memory!'

Preston considered her for a moment. She had once been pretty in an unremarkable mousy style; now that had faded, leaving her with a washed out look that matched her timid air. She was kind and gentle, but such qualities did not appeal to a full blooded gentleman like his master. He knew a great deal about Sir Aubrey's private life, as was only likely after more than twenty years in his service. Preston knew, too, how to be discreet.

He shook his head.

'No, milady. Before he set out for White's yesterday morning, he informed me that he would be dining at Carlton House in the evening. I accordingly laid out his dinner dress in readiness, but he did not return here to change.'

Her eyes opened wide at this.

'Oh, dear! Dining with the Prince at Carlton House, you say? But he would most certainly need to change into evening dress for that! And you've had no message?'

'I am afraid not, milady. But, of course, it's still early in the day.'

She breathed a sigh of relief. 'Ten o'clock – oh, yes, of course it is! No doubt we shall hear later. Thank you, Preston.'

'Milady.'

The valet withdrew.

Lady Jermyn mentioned her husband's unexplained absence to her niece by marriage, Charlotte Jermyn, when the latter came into the morning room. Charlotte, a lively blonde with a smile that captured most male hearts, gave a tiny shrug.

'Well, yes, Aunt, it *is* unusual, I know, but emergencies do sometimes occur. I don't mean,' she added hastily, seeing a look of apprehension cross Lady Jermyn's countenance, 'anything in the nature of an accident. My uncle is too well-known for us not to be informed of such a thing immediately. But perhaps some urgent matter of business – you're certain no word has come from Sussex to send him dashing off to Wynsfield?'

Lady Jermyn shook her head. 'He would never have gone without Preston,' she said, decidedly. 'Besides, why could he not leave me a message with one of the servants?'

'Pray don't vex yourself, my love,' advised Miss Jermyn, with an air of one twice her years. 'He'll appear presently, you will see. I mean to go shopping this morning – do you wish to come?'

The afternoon still brought no news of the master of the

house; and Lady Jermyn was hard put to it to know what to say when one of his friends called later with the intention of giving him a lift to an arranged meeting with some others.

'I'm vastly sorry, Mr Ambrose,' she said, falteringly, 'but my husband is not here at present.'

The Honourable Nigel Ambrose raised his neatly plucked eyebrows and stared at her.

'Not here, ma'am? Then – pardon me – where the dooce is he? We're engaged to Winters for this evening – made the arrangements at White's last Friday. Only four days ago – can't have forgotten. Yes, and another thing,' he went on, his indignation mounting. 'He wasn't at Carlton House yesterday evening. Tell you what, ma'am, his credit with Prinney must be better than mine, to miss a Royal dinner without a word of apology. Doing it too brown, if you ask me. Not ill, is he?'

'N-no,' stammered Lady Jermyn. 'That is – not exactly.' She gazed about her wildly for inspiration, then Charlotte's words came into her mind. 'He's had to go down to Wynsfield, our house in Sussex,' she finished, with a desperate swallow. 'An urgent matter of business. You will understand, sir, I'm sure. He – he asked me to apologise.'

'Hmph!' exclaimed Mr Ambrose, in far from satisfied tones. 'Must say, it seems a havey cavey business to me – beg your pardon, ma'am, but it ain't like Jermyn to cut and run like this, giving all his appointments the go by. Not a punctilious feller exactly, but one always knows where one is with him. Still, mustn't take up any more of your time. I'll explain to Winters. 'Servant, Lady Jermyn.'

After he had left, she cast herself wearily into a chair; and it was there that Charlotte found her, when the girl had returned from a drive in the Park with one of her admirers.

'What am I to do, Lottie dear?' she wailed, having explained what had happened.

'If this isn't just like Uncle Aubrey!' exclaimed Charlotte, bitterly.

'Oh, no, how can you say so? I can't recall a single previous occasion when he has absented himself without ensuring that I had due warning. It's not in the *least* like him! That's what is so worrying.'

'I mean it's like him not to care a rush for anyone else's feelings, but just to consider what *he* wants,' replied her niece, somewhat illogically. 'I tell you what, Aunt Amelia, if it weren't for making you unhappy, I'd as lief he took himself off for good!'

'Oh, no, dearest, really you mustn't say such things! I know you're vexed with him because he is trying to persuade you to wed Lord Escott, but only consider how your welfare has always been his first concern ever since you were placed in our charge as a baby scarce three years old, poor little mite! What a darling you were – I loved you on sight, just as if you were my own – indeed, I feel that you truly are!'

Charlotte gave her a warm embrace.

'I know, my love, and so do I. But as for my uncle, whenever I see anyone but himself being his first concern, why, pigs may fly! I'm a wretch to upset you, though,' she added contritely. 'Don't regard my sharp tongue – dare say I shall turn out to be the most odious shrew, then no one will wish to marry me. Not that I care a rush for that at present, for I've only just begun to enjoy myself with balls and parties and the like, and it would be a pity to settle down too soon.'

Her aunt wagged her head sagely.

'Ah, that's because Mr Right hasn't chanced along! Only wait, and you will see!'

Charlotte laughed.

The following day, Lady Jermyn sent Preston off to Sussex to see if his master had indeed gone to their country house. He returned late in the evening to report that the servants at Wynsfield had not seen Sir Aubrey since the family's last visit in March and moreover had no notion of his present whereabouts.

Seriously alarmed now, Lady Jermyn tried to consider what was best to be done. To raise a public hue and cry was out of the question, for nothing would anger her husband more when he finally returned home. She had no close relatives living in London whom she might have consulted, and she did not wish to burden Charlotte, who should be enjoying herself, with anxiety.

She waited patiently for one more day, then finally succumbed to the temptation to confide in someone outside the family. She had for many years been friendly with Lady Quainton, a widow of ample means who had also been a close friend of Anthea Rutherford's dead grandmother. Charlotte had gone riding in the park with a group of other young people, leaving her aunt free to follow her own devices for a few hours. Trusting to luck that Lady Quainton would be at home that morning, Lady Jermyn called at her friend's house in Grosvenor Square.

Fortune favoured her. There were no other callers with Cassandra Quainton, neither was her friend about to set out on any necessary expedition. She was a shrewd, though compassionate observer, and soon saw that Amelia Jermyn was very unhappy and disturbed.

She ordered some coffee in spite of her visitor's refusal, and talked quietly of trivialities until they were served and once more alone.

'Drink it, my dear, and then tell me what is weighing on your mind. It's of no use to say that there's nothing,' she added, anticipating resistance, 'for I can see quite well that you're in a sad taking.'

But Amelia Jermyn had no will to offer resistance. She unfolded her tale, a little incoherently, for she herself was uncertain of the facts.

'I am to understand, then, that your husband walked out of the house on Monday as usual to go to White's, and has not been seen since? And you've received no word from him?' summarised Lady Quainton, in calm tones.

'Yes, oh, yes! Is it not dreadful? And I don't at all know what to do, my dear Cassandra,' said Lady Jermyn, going through the motions of what is generally called wringing the hands.

'You're quite certain that,' said Lady Quainton, delicately, 'there is no little – ah – peccadillo – to account for his absence? Gentlemen sometimes – you'll pardon me for presuming on a long friendship to suggest such a thing, I'm sure – *do* stray from the straight and narrow path, vanishing from their homes mysteriously for a little while?'

Her friend flushed uncomfortably. 'He has never before gone anywhere without letting me know where he may be found, or without taking Preston, his valet. I know what you mean, and I am not saying that there *may* not have been instances when – but, in short, he has never absented himself in this way before.'

Lady Quainton reflected that after all there were ample opportunities for gentlemen to pursue extra-marital relationships without being so blatant about it as to disappear without warning.

'You could go to the magistrates at Bow Street,' she suggested. 'It is a part of their business to find missing persons of the Quality.'

Lady Jermyn exclaimed in horror. 'Oh, no! It would inevitably start a scandal if official inquiries were set on foot! And should Aubrey return with some perfectly ordinary reason for his absence, nothing would infuriate him more than to find I had made a stir! Of all things, he abominates fuss of any kind!'

'So do most gentlemen. But you cannot go on like this, Amelia, worrying yourself to death until he chooses to let you know where he is. Some discreet inquiries must be made, and I think I know the very person to carry them out to perfection, could I but persuade him to interest himself in the affair. Let me explain a little.'

CHAPTER II

On that same morning, the Honourable Justin Rutherford had returned to his bachelor rooms in Albemarle Street after an absence of more than a month spent in pursuing his antiquarian interests.

His rumpled dark hair, negligently tied cravat and casual style of dress suggested neither the prosy antiquary nor the fashionable sprig of the *ton.* Nevertheless, he had published a book on the antiquities of Greece a few years since which had earned him academic respect; and he was known to defend the seventh Earl of Elgin's action in bringing to England priceless sculptures from the ancient Greek temple, the Parthenon, so that they might be preserved from the depredations of the Turks who were in power there.

As for fashion, his tailoring was good and he could look presentable enough when he chose. But although he took an interest in most sporting pursuits, rarely did he grace the drawing rooms of the *ton.* Matchmaking mamas had more or less given him up, but still gilt edged invitation cards continued to arrive regularly.

He was gazing at a pile of these now, in some dismay, when a welcome interruption occurred.

'Lady Quainton has called, sir,' announced his man, Selby.

Justin tossed the cards aside, closed the lid of the

bureau, and rose to his feet.

'Splendid!' he exclaimed. 'Pray admit her at once.'

Lady Quainton appeared, elegant as always, in a walking dress of grey silk and a tall crowned bonnet with ostrich plumes. He took a quick step towards her, both arms outstretched.

'You're quick off the mark, Godmama!' he exclaimed, giving her a filial hug. 'I've been home scarce half a day! Not bad news, I trust, that brings you hotfoot?'

She returned his embrace warmly. 'No, no, my dear Justin, nothing of the kind. But I did feel that perhaps I should lose no time in seeing you, for you're so elusive, you might be off to the other side of the universe before I could put on my bonnet.'

He regarded her quizzically, indicating that she should be seated.

'Sounds dashed smoky to me,' he said, with a grin. 'I'd lay any odds you've something in mind for me to do. Confess it, now – but first, what shall I order for you? Tea, coffee, ratafia, lemonade? How vastly agreeable it is to see you, when I was about to spend a dreary hour with my accumulated correspondence. What will you take, ma'am?'

'Nothing, I thank you, for it's not long since I was taking coffee with Amelia Jermyn,' she answered. Then, quickly adopting the direct approach which she knew he favoured – 'That's what I wished to see you about, Justin. Poor Amelia's almost beside herself with worry – her husband's disappeared. He walked out of the house on Monday morning, and has not been seen since.'

Justin raised his brows. 'Jermyn? I know the fellow by sight, of course – one of Prinney's set, ain't he? Odd fish, many of 'em – not much in my style. In what way did you suppose I might advise?'

She gave him a sideways look.

'Well, I *did* hope – that's to say, it seemed to me you are the very person to discover what's befallen him without creating the kind of scandal my friend so much dreads. And rightly, for so would I, in her place.'

'There's usually one quite simple explanation for a disappearance of that kind, dear ma'am,' answered Justin, with a wry twist of his lips.

'I know, but Amelia insists that her husband has never before absented himself without leaving word where he may be found, or, indeed, without taking his valet. One knows from gossip that he has a roving eye, but it's plain from what she tells me that he doesn't conduct his liaisons in that headlong style. There can be no doubt that he has vanished into thin air, so to speak; and, knowing how a mystery intrigues you, I thought of you at once.'

Curiosity being also an integral part of the academic mind, Justin had his fair share, like his niece Anthea. He gave a considering frown.

'Two other possible explanations, then. The first is what happened to the unfortunate Brummell a few weeks since – flight to France to escape creditors.'

'Oh, no, nothing of that kind! Jermyn is tolerably plump in the pocket, as anyone may see. No expense spared either in the Town house or at Wynsfield, his Sussex residence, and Amelia and Charlotte always turned out in the first style of elegance! He's a regular devotee of the Turf and the tables, with never a hint of financial embarrassments.'

'Hm.' In spite of himself, Justin's interest was beginning to be engaged. 'An accident to someone as well known as a member of Prinney's set would of course be quickly reported. But just suppose it wasn't an ordinary kind of accident? There was a fellow officer in Spain, once, when I was out there with Wellington – he took a crack on the pate and lost all account of himself for several days. Odd circumstance, but the medicos seemed familiar with it. Not that I favour an explanation of so dramatic a kind – bound to be a simpler one.'

She looked thoughtful. 'Now that *does* seem within the bounds of possibility, dramatic or no. But surely if such a mischance should have occurred, he would be wandering about where someone would be certain to recognise him? As you say, he's a well known member of the *ton*, and that's a small world, after all.'

'He may not be wandering loose,' murmured Justin, frowning. 'There are a number of other possibilities – ' He broke off. 'The thing would be, to discover when and where he was last seen, and by whom. But I'm not at all sure that I wish to meddle,' he added. 'It would mean a deuced lot of prying into the fellow's private concerns – he'd scarce thank me, if he turned up in the end all right and tight, which I dare say he may do.'

Lady Quainton rested an urgent hand on his sleeve for a moment.

'That's precisely what prevents Amelia Jermyn from appealing to Bow Street, a course which I suggested to her. But if the situation continues, it may come to that, and she certainly feels that it would be more agreeable to have one of her husband's own social standing to make inquiries.'

'Then why not one of his intimate friends?'

'Ah, well, you see, she made an unfortunate blunder in that regard. She did it for the best, as one often does. When one of his friends came asking for him the day after he disappeared, she said he'd been sent for to their property in Sussex on urgent business. She is not very closely acquainted with any of his particular set, so dislikes the notion of telling them the truth and asking for their help. She would even prefer a comparative stranger, like yourself, odd though you may think it. Though, after all,' she mused, 'it's extraordinary how people frequently *do* confide in total strangers. Especially when travelling.'

Justin nodded. 'Noticed it myself. Well, since you insist, you may take me to call on the lady, and we'll see what transpires. I make no promises, mind.'

'Oh, by the way,' added Lady Quainton, as she rose. 'I forgot to mention that she has a most charming niece by marriage who is Jermyn's ward. Her name is Charlotte, and so far she is unattached, though I understand her uncle has been trying to promote a match between her and Escott.'

'Escott – that ancient roué?' demanded Justin scornfully. 'How old is she, then, this female? Is she an antidote?'

'I told you,' replied Lady Quainton, with some indignation, 'she's a vastly attractive girl of Anthea's age, or thereabouts. But you'll meet her for yourself, and then you may judge.'

Justin caught her eye, and she looked a little conscious. He laughed, and flicked her cheek with his finger.

'Oh, Godmama, when will you give up matchmaking on my behalf?' he quizzed.

Nevertheless, he had to admit to himself later that Miss Charlotte Jermyn was, in the slang phraseology, very well to pass. Blue-eyed blondes were by no means uncommon, but they did tend to have vapid expressions. This one possessed a pert little nose, a sparkle in her eye and a humorous mouth. His eyes met hers in a glance of open appreciation as they were introduced.

For her part, she was somewhat intrigued by this alert looking gentleman who wore his good tailoring with an easy air and whose manner, though never seeking to impress and at times bordering on the flippant, yet conveyed a sense of assurance and quiet authority. She stole a second glance at him under her eyelids. He was not exactly *handsome*, she reflected, but he had an interesting, attractive face.

Somewhat to her chagrin, he caught her scrutiny and responded with a half grin.

'It's odd that we've never chanced to meet before, Mr Rutherford,' said Lady Jermyn, 'since I'm acquainted with your relatives, Viscount and Lady Rutherford.'

'And Anthea's a friend of mine,' put in Charlotte, before he could answer. 'I collect she must be your – ' She paused, struck by the incongruity of it – 'your *niece*?'

He gave a broad smile. 'Absurd, is it not? But I promise you she shows me scant respect – not that I look for any.'

She laughed softly, and he thought her enchanting.

'Your years are at fault, sir. Now, if you were a greybeard – '

He joined in her laughter for a moment, before turning to Lady Jermyn in a more sober mood.

'You won't encounter me about Town a great deal, ma'am. I live a somewhat nomadic life, I fear. But I collect that at present you're seriously disturbed by your husband's unexplained absence, and would like me to try what I can discover in that regard?'

She clasped her hands together in a gesture of supplication.

'Oh, if only you would, I should be forever in your debt! Cassandra – that is, your godmother – says you are very clever at solving mysteries, and indeed I have heard something myself – '

She broke off and shuddered, evidently reluctant to follow such a melancholy train of thought as the late Marmaduke Yarnton's murder.

'I am persuaded that something unusual must have befallen him,' she continued, 'for otherwise he would never leave me in ignorance of his whereabouts in this heartless way! At the same time, I don't wish to bring officials into the matter, for if in the end it turns out to be nothing, he would be prodigiously vexed!'

Justin nodded. 'I quite understand, and need scarce say that I'd be happy to serve you, Lady Jermyn. But I would first like you to consider that any kind of inquiry may possibly stray into personal concerns which could distress either your husband or yourself. Obviously, it would be better in the hands of a male relative rather than an outsider like myself. I collect from Lady Quainton that you don't care to ask any of your husband's friends, but is there no one else?'

'No, there is no one.' Lady Jermyn's lips trembled. 'My husband's brother – Charlotte's father – is dead, and I have no close relatives on my side. I have indeed considered everything you say, sir, and it can make no difference, for I can no longer go on in this way! The uncertainty is killing me by inches!'

She bowed her head in her hands, giving way to her grief. Charlotte was beside her in an instant, enfolding her in loving arms and turning an eloquent look of pleading upon Justin.

'Pray do consent to help us, sir! We realise that we are asking a prodigious favour, for why should you embroil yourself in our concerns, unconnected with us as you are? But we would be so vastly grateful – oh, I don't know how to find the right words – but please – please!'

She sounded like a small child in deep trouble; and her countenance was even lovelier, he thought, when touched by emotion.

He smiled gently. 'How could I possibly refuse, ma'am? I should be a veritable monster! Very well, I'll do my possible.'

'Oh, thank you, thank you!' she exclaimed, with sparkling eyes.

'Possibly when Lady Jermyn is more composed,' he

said, quietly, 'I might put a few questions to you both? Lady Quainton has already repeated to me everything which was confided to her, but it's always valuable to have a first-hand account. And if neither of you ladies would object, I'd prefer to question you separately. It's important to have *unprompted* recollections, as I believe you'll readily see.'

Charlotte nodded, quick to understand, as he had known she would be. Once she and Lady Quainton had soothed Lady Jermyn into a more equable state of mind, they both withdrew to the far end of the drawing room, out of earshot though not out of sight, so that Justin might converse with her alone.

A few tactful questions soon showed him that there was nothing new to be learnt from her. Jermyn had left home on Monday morning with the declared intention of going to White's and of dining later in the day with the Prince Regent. It was now Friday, and nothing had been heard of him.

He thanked Lady Jermyn and she rose to sit at the other end of the room beside Lady Quainton, Charlotte taking her place opposite Justin.

He regarded Miss Jermyn in silence for several minutes, until she raised her eyebrows at him quizzically. He seemed to be deep in thought; but in reality he was appreciating the charming picture she presented in her white muslin gown sprigged with tiny pink rosebuds, and the pink ribbon threaded through her yellow curls.

He coughed slightly, jerking himself out of this pleasant reverie to the business at hand.

'I'd like you to be frank with me if you will, Miss Jermyn,' he began. 'Have you any notion at all as to where your uncle may be? I can quite see that there could be reasons why you should keep any such surmises from

Lady Jermyn, but unless I can have your full confidence, it will be difficult for me to assist you.'

She nodded. 'Yes, of course I realise that, Mr Rutherford, and therefore I'll say *in confidence* what I would otherwise be unwilling to mention. The truth is that my aunt and uncle have little in common, and merely try to support the usual observances of marriage. Possibly there's nothing so unusual in that,' she put in, cynically. 'But it's certainly true that he does always inform her of his absences from home, even if he doesn't trouble himself to state exactly where he's going. He has never stayed away before like this.'

'And you can't hazard a guess as to where he may be?'

She hesitated for a moment, avoiding his eyes, then she tilted her chin and faced him resolutely.

'Not precisely, no. But wherever he may be, I'll be bound there's a female concerned! There, you asked for frankness,' she concluded, defiantly, 'and now you have it. Doubtless you think me vastly improper, and undutiful into the bargain, but if you desire the truth, that cannot be helped!'

'No such thing,' he replied, smiling at her in a disarming way. 'On the contrary, I am grateful that you found the courage to speak your mind. You cannot go further, and suggest a likely place, or a – particular companion?'

She shook her head. 'I'm sorry, but I cannot help you there. Do you suppose – ' her expression sobered – 'that something untoward can have happened to him? It seems so very unlike him to have broken an engagement to dine with the Prince Regent – I need scarce tell you that no one dares behave in that way! And moreover, he is one of the Prince's close circle. I must admit that I have no particular fondness for my uncle – he has never shown the least consideration for me, and of late he's been trying to force me into a hateful marriage! But all the same, for my aunt's sake, I wouldn't wish him to come to any harm.'

'Do you know of anyone who might wish him harm, Miss Rutherford?'

She considered this for a moment.

'Well, no,' she said, slowly. 'At least, unless the husbands of some of his inamoratas – but that is *too* melodramatic! He may have enemies, but not to that degree!'

He nodded. No need to embarrass her by asking for names; he could doubtless obtain the information from his godmother, who always knew the Town gossip.

He thanked her, and reluctantly turned away to ask Lady Jermyn if he might interview the valet.

'I'd prefer to see him on his own ground, ma'am, if you don't object,' he said. 'Perhaps in your husband's dressing room?'

She looked surprised, but agreed; and soon Preston was confronting him in the small room which led off Sir Aubrey Jermyn's bedchamber.

'I understand that Sir Aubrey left the house on Monday with the intention of going to White's Club,' began Justin. 'Did he positively state this?'

'He said he would be looking in at White's, sir, but the remark was merely dropped, so to speak.'

'He also told you that he'd be dining at Carlton House that evening?'

'That is correct, sir. I laid out his dress clothes in the usual way, but he never returned to change.'

'Did you not think this sufficiently unusual to draw Lady Jermyn's attention to it?'

Preston coughed. 'Her ladyship was at a private ball that evening with Miss Jermyn. Besides, I wasn't wishful of doing anything which – ' he hesitated.

'Which would annoy or embarrass your master?' put in Justin, quickly.

'Yes, sir, that was it.'

'Had Sir Aubrey ever before failed to return home without warning?'

'No, sir. And if he was staying anywhere away from home, he would always take me with him. That's what I can't understand, sir. Besides, he has taken no clothes with him, not even an overnight bag.'

Justin nodded thoughtfully.

'I believe you went down to his house in Sussex to make inquiries. Did you learn anything there to the purpose?'

'Indeed not, sir. None of the servants had set eyes on him since the family's last visit in March, when I accompanied them. There had been no communication except for the usual small, everyday matters of business between the estate agent, Mr Hawthorn, and Sir Aubrey. No mention of another visit, sir.'

'But I think,' Justin said, persuasively, 'that you may possibly have some notion yourself about your master's disappearance. You've been twenty years in his employ, I collect – long enough to gain some insight into his private concerns. There may be matters which you don't care to mention to my lady personally, but I know she has impressed upon you the importance of concealing nothing from me. Come, now. Perhaps it will help you if I say at once that I know of Sir Aubrey's reputation as a lady's man.'

Preston's expression lightened. 'Well, sir, if it's to be plain dealing,' he said, in a confidential tone, 'I may be able to show you something, though I fear it won't help much. As you say, sir, the master did have his fancies in the petticoat line, and I couldn't help but know about most of them. Indeed, half the Town knew, too, for he was – '

'One moment,' interrupted Justin, sharply. 'I notice you're using the past tense when you speak of Sir Aubrey. Why?'

The valet seemed nonplussed for a moment.

'Well, Mr Rutherford, it's just a manner of speaking, I suppose, thinking back on times past. I can't rightly account for it, sir.'

'No matter. You were saying – ?'

'What was I saying? Oh, yes, that Sir Aubrey has never troubled to conceal his affaires, until recently. Lately there's been someone to whom any breath of scandal would be fatal, by my reckoning, for everything's been conducted in a more havey cavey style, if you take my meaning.'

Justin nodded. 'What was it you wished to show me?'

Preston stepped over to a wardrobe, took from it a frogged red silk dressing robe, and removed a slip of paper from one of the pockets.

'I'd forgotten about this until now, sir,' he said, handing it to Justin.

Justin unfolded it carefully. As he did so, a faint aroma of attar of roses wafted to his nostrils. The message it contained was brief, and in a hasty but indisputably feminine hand.

I will be at the usual rendezvous on Monday between two and three o'clock. My dearest love – S.

He studied it for several minutes.

'I found it when I was hanging up the garment,' explained the valet, a shade defensively. 'I felt the crackle of paper and opened it, thinking it of no importance since it wasn't sealed or enclosed in any way. Sir Aubrey was out at the time, so I replaced it, then forgot all about it.'

'When did you find this?'

'Last Saturday morning, sir, when I was tidying in here as usual.'

'And have you any notion who the sender – the cryptic 'S' – may be? Don't be afraid to answer, for it may lead us to Sir Aubrey.'

The valet shook his head. 'I fear not, sir. I told you that

this affaire has been conducted with the utmost discretion, so that even I have never gained the least hint as to the lady's identity. All I can say with certainty is that it started about the time that the family returned in March from Wynsfield – Sir Aubrey's residence in Sussex, you know, sir. There have been other messages, though naturally I've never before read them. I saw the master burn one, once, at the candle. And there've been other little signs, easy to follow when you're serving a gentleman day and night. All I can say is, he's never been so particular about secrecy before, but I can't tell who the lady may be.'

'H'm.' Justin raised the note to his nostrils and sniffed delicately at it. 'I shall keep this,' he said decisively, taking out his pocket book and stowing the paper away inside it. 'In the meantime, should anything else occur to you which may assist in discovering Sir Aubrey, be good enough to report to me. Here's my card.'

He handed a calling card to Preston, who accepted it with a bow before showing him the way back to the drawing room.

CHAPTER III

The following morning, Justin made tactful inquiries at White's and other clubs known to be patronised by Jermyn. He elicited the information that Sir Aubrey had not entered any of their premises on the previous Monday; and, furthermore, no one seemed to have set eyes on him at all that day.

Already a vague rumour was beginning to circulate, started by the Honourable Nigel Ambrose's account of the shabby way in which Jermyn had broken all his engagements without so much as a word of apology and dashed off to his place in Sussex.

'And I tell you what,' concluded Ambrose darkly to a few of his cronies, 'Prinney is seriously annoyed.'

They shook their heads gravely.

'Devilish stupid way to behave,' pronounced one. 'Not likely he'll ever win his way back into favour after what amounts to a monstrous slight. Remember how Brummell cooked his goose some time back – before he got into deep water and had to cut and run to Calais – by offering Prinney some damned sarcastic remarks? Can't treat a Prince of the Realm in that fashion, favourite or no.'

Fortunately, however, this topic was so far quite eclipsed by other, more juicy pieces of gossip. Foremost among these in both the clubs and the drawing rooms was the scandalous book *Glenarvon* which had just been published. Its author was the now notorious Lady Caroline Lamb; and it revived all the old scandals concerning Lord Byron which had provided the caricaturists and print shops with such gratifying profits in recent months, until the furore had finally driven the poet out of England for good.

'She's gone her length now,' declared Lady Holland. 'Her characters are easily identified with members of the *ton* – The Duchess of Devonshire, Lady Jersey, Lady Granville – and of course, Byron himself. She's even had the monstrous audacity to publish some of the actual love letters he wrote to her! Mark my words, she'll live to regret writing such a piece of scurrilous nonsense! Though,' she added, on a more pragmatic note, 'they say the sales of the book are prodigious.'

Having returned from his unprofitable excursion into St James's Street, Justin decided to look in at his brother's house in Berkeley Square. He was greeted with enthusiasm.

'This is capital, old fellow! Where the deuce have you been this time? Must say, you look more like an Ethiopian than an honest Englishman with that devilish tanned countenance – fetching to the females, though, I'll wager!'

'I've been taking a look at some of the prehistoric burial chambers scattered about this country,' explained Justin, stretching out his long legs in a chair and accepting the offer of a glass of wine. 'Fascinating places, y'know – might put together a book on 'em, sometime.'

'Burial chambers! Good God, man, you'll find plenty to fascinate you here in Town, I'll be bound, and something that's living and breathing, too! You're a devilish queer fish, Justin, damme if you ain't. Don't know where you get it from – no scholars in our family that I know of – certainly not myself! They only got me through Eton by tanning my hide regularly, give you my word.'

Justin grinned. 'Doing it too brown, Ned. You're not quite the addlepate you'd like to be thought. Besides, you're forgetting our maternal grandfather Anderson and his brother the Bishop. Cambridge men, it's true,' he added, with the natural bias of an Oxford graduate, 'but reputable scholars, in spite of that, and friends of William Stukeley.'

Edward frowned. 'Stukeley? Now, who the devil – '

'Antiquarian. Wrote several books on the subject, including a useful study of Avebury and Stonehenge, although the historian Gibbon repudiates much of his information as fanciful speculation.'

Edward flung up his arms in a gesture of surrender. 'Spare me, young 'un! How long a stay do you mean to make in Town this time, eh?'

'No saying.' Justin shrugged.

Edward gave him an envious look. 'Nice to be footloose, with no ties of family or estate.'

'Sometimes – very well, most of the time. That's what comes of being the youngest member of the family, old chap. Tell me, how do your family go on? Elizabeth's well, I trust? And my irrepressible niece Anthea? Not to mention the boys.'

'M'wife's in her usual good health, I'm glad to say, and the boys ain't been expelled from Eton yet, though there's no saying what may happen, young devils! As for Anthea, suitors flock round her like bees round a honeypot, but can I get her off my hands? Devil a bit of it! Too choosy by half, give you my word!'

Presently they joined Lady Rutherford and Anthea for an informal luncheon of cold meats and fruit.

'I hear you're conducting yourself in your usual style,' Justin remarked to his niece in a low tone. 'Breaking hearts right and left without mercy. Your papa tells me he quite despairs of ever seeing you off.'

Her hazel eyes twinkled. 'A fine one you are to talk such fustian to me! What of your own amorous exploits, I'd like to know? Surely someone must by now have pointed out to you the desirability of settling down with one of the many prodigiously lovely, talented and eligible young ladies at present doing the season in Town? And you so stricken in years, too – I wonder you don't take warning that it may very soon be too late! But don't despair – I'll stand your friend, and put you in the way of meeting some of them. Only give me the word!'

'You are very good.' He sketched a mock bow. 'And should I ever require a marriage broker, you of course would inevitably spring to mind. By the way,' he added, with a change of tone, 'I collect you are acquainted with Miss Charlotte Jermyn?'

She chuckled. ' "Oho, sits the wind in that quarter?" – as they say in Covent Garden melodramas. Charlotte – yes, she *is* rather a dear, and might suit you very well, now I think of it. That's to say, unless that wretched uncle of hers succeeds in forcing her into marriage with *Lord Escott*, of all odious men! But she declares she never, never will consent, and I fancy he'll have hard work of it, for Charlotte is no meek Bath miss, but a sensible female with a mind of her own!' She broke off. 'But why do you mention her? Have you two chanced to meet? Do you like her?'

'The answer to the first is in the affirmative, and to the second – ' he eyed her with a grin – 'that I find her tolerable.'

'*Tolerable*!' she repeated, in disgust. 'Now I know that there is positively no hope for you!'

'No, do you think so? I dare say you are right. But don't you wish to hear how I became acquainted with your paragon?'

She turned a face alive with curiosity towards him, so that he could not help laughing aloud.

'It was really my godmother's doing,' he began.

She nodded wisely. 'Ah, yes, Lady Quainton has always wished to see you established with a suitable wife,' she said, mocking him.

'Quite so. But on this occasion, she was desirous of engaging my interest on Lady Jermyn's behalf, not that of her niece. It seems that Jermyn has vanished, leaving his wife in some anxiety as to his whereabouts. Godmama thought I might be able to assist in tracing him.'

'Heard of that at White's,' put in Edward. 'Went off to his place in Sussex in a hurry last Monday, so they say, breaking all his engagements, including one with Prinney, with never a word of apology. Deuced shabby thing to do – something smoky there, to my way of thinking. No man in his senses behaves like that.'

Justin shook his head.

'That's the story Lady Jermyn put about, but it's not accurate. It was the best she could think of at short notice when confronted by one of his friends in a pelter because Jermyn had broken an engagement with him. Bound to be discredited in time, too, should anyone go seeking him out in Sussex. The truth is simply, as I said, that the man's vanished. No one's set eyes on him since Monday morning, when he left home, ostensibly to go to White's.'

Anthea, who had been listening to all this in mounting excitement, shook her head vigorously. 'Oh, but someone *has* – me!' she declared, with a fine disregard for the lessons in grammar painstakingly delivered in the past by her governess. 'I saw him – on Monday afternoon at Madame Yvonne's! And, oh, Justin, I thought at the time that it would turn out to be tame, you know, as most seemingly exciting things do! But now it looks as though it may be part of a famous mystery, after all! I was never so delighted!'

'*You saw him*?' queried Justin, turning an alert glance

upon her. 'At Madame Yvonne's, you say? Who is this good lady, and where does she reside?'

Anthea chuckled. 'Oh, she's not a good lady – at least, not in that sense, though I'm quite sure she leads a blameless life. That's part of the mystery, in fact, for one cannot at all credit that Madame is conducting a – '

She broke off, seeing her mother's warning eye upon her, and coughed delicately.

'For pity's sake, Anthea, give me a round tale!' pleaded Justin, throwing up his hands in a gesture of disgust. 'You'd better tell me the whole – start at the beginning.'

Thus encouraged, she did so; and though her parents tut-tutted a little at the recital of her impulsive intrusion into the modiste's privacy, their disapproval was fairly indulgent for once.

'I'm bound to say,' corroborated Lady Rutherford, when Anthea had rounded off the account with her speculations on the subject, 'that it's most improbable that Madame should be involved in any illicit liaison. She is a female who thinks first and foremost of her business concerns, and any breath of scandal would affect those adversely, as anyone must realise. Besides, she's past the age for romantical fancies.'

'Is any female past that age?' demanded her husband, laughing.

'You may choose to make game,' said his wife, severely, 'but I assure you that Madame Yvonne is as hard headed a business woman as I know of, besides not being at all the kind of female to attract a man of Jermyn's stamp.'

'But if he were not there for that reason, then what else could it be?' asked Edward, now as intrigued as his daughter.

'Well, he certainly seemed to be waiting for somebody,' replied Anthea, slowly.

'He was,' declared Justin. 'And you're quite right in

thinking it was not for the proprietress of the shop – unless I'm much mistaken. Tell me, oh my observant niece, was there any other customer on the premises at the same time as yourself?'

'Oh, yes, there was that tiresome Lady Deanesford – *you* know, Mama! She's a vastly talkative female, Justin, and she quite took up all Yvonne's attention, which is why I think I came to be shown into that little room by mistake, because Yvonne had to leave me to an assistant, instead of looking after me herself, as she usually does.'

Lady Rutherford said that indeed she did know of Lady Deanesford's shortcomings.

'Does this Lady Deanesford chance to have a baptismal name beginning with the letter "S"?' asked Justin.

Anthea looked intrigued, but shook her head to indicate that she did not know. Her mother answered for her.

'No, she is Lucretia Eleanor. She was a Henshawe, you know, and came out in the same year as I did, though we were never close friends.'

'Then she's not the lady concerned,' said Justin, decisively.

'What do you mean?' demanded Anthea, now agog with curiosity. 'Justin, you know something that I do not! It's a great deal too bad of you to keep it a secret – pray tell me at once, or I have done with you for ever!'

'Anthea!' exclaimed Lady Rutherford, in shocked tones. 'Will you be pleased to try for a little more conduct? Even in the bosom of the family, it is scarce proper for you to be discussing such subjects, leave alone displaying a vulgar curiosity over something which *your uncle* – ' she stressed the words – 'thinks fit to conceal from you. You are going beyond the line of what is pleasing, miss!'

'Your mama is quite in the right of it,' said her father, with commendable firmness. 'All the same, Justin – '

turning to his brother in a confidential way – 'no reason why you can't tell *me* privately, is there?'

Anthea looked crestfallen, but her parents were not deceived. They had long ago given up all hope of turning their mercurial daughter into the usual pattern of a well bred young lady of Quality. Secretly, they were extremely fond of her just as she was.

By the slightest flicker of his eyelid, Justin managed to convey to her that all was not lost. She rose from the table with her mama, looking so unnaturally demure that her father burst out laughing, and declared she was an incorrigible little puss.

It was not until later that Anthea found an opportunity to confer with Justin alone. Lady Rutherford had gone up to her room to recoup her energies for the evening's junketings, while Anthea's father had been called away for a few moments from the bookroom, where he had been closeted with his younger brother. Seizing her opportunity, Anthea slipped quickly into the room, closing the door softly behind her.

'Justin, quick!' she commanded, in a low tone. 'Tell me what it is!'

'Your mother is quite right, of course,' he replied with a teasing grin. 'It's not a fitting subject for your shell-like ears. However – ' he drew out his pocket book and abstracted the note which he had obtained from Preston – 'since neither of your parents can assist me in identifying the writer of this *billet doux*, perhaps you can.'

She took the note in an eager hand, swiftly scanning its contents.

'So that's the significance of the initial "S" for you,' she said. 'I'm more than ever certain that it can't be Madame Yvonne. Even allowing for the fact that her real name most likely is not Yvonne, she wouldn't have phrased her summons in quite that way, I think. "At the usual rendezvous" suggests somewhere other than one's own premises, don't you agree?'

Justin nodded. 'So I would suppose. But the modiste must be involved in some way, or Jermyn wouldn't be able to make use of her premises for his assignations. What is more important, however, is to establish the identity of "S". Your mother points out – rightly – that there are scores of feminine names beginning with that letter. I had hoped that she might have been able to identify the handwriting from signed invitation cards and so on which she might have received at some time or other, but no such luck. Can you do so?'

He realised as he asked that this was far less likely, as Anthea would not receive as many invitation cards as her mama.

She shook her head, a disappointed look in her eyes, and was silent for a moment.

'In view of this note, I've been assuming that you saw Jermyn between the hours mentioned. Is that correct?' resumed Justin.

'Yes. I must have arrived about a quarter after two, I think. I wasn't there long – not more than half an hour.'

'And you're quite sure that no other client than this Lady Deanesford was there at the same time as yourself?'

'Yes, quite sure,' she corroborated, then stopped. 'Wait a moment, though,' she continued in mounting excitement. 'No one else was actually *in* the showroom, but someone did arrive just as I was leaving – Viscountess St Clare! Mama has only a slight acquaintance with her, so we merely bowed in passing. But I don't at all know what her first names may be, and I doubt if Mama does, either. I tell you what, though, Justin – I'm sure I can soon discover that! Yes, and what's more,' she went on, reaching a crescendo of enthusiasm, 'if you'll only entrust that note to me, I dare say I may find an opportunity to compare it with a sample of her handwriting!'

He regarded her suspiciously. 'How do you propose to set about that?'

'Oh, plenty of other people receive invitation cards, for one thing,' she replied, airily. 'I might find out who has had one from her, and then cajole the recipient into giving me a sight of it. Or there may be another way of achieving my object. Spontaneity is often the best guide to success, don't you agree?'

'In you it's frequently the signpost to disaster,' he said, darkly. 'Well, if I do entrust this to you, will you promise not to get yourself into a scrape of any kind? I wouldn't for one moment agree to the scheme, but that I feel my own chance of attempting the kind of thing you have in mind is remote. My credit with my small – but interesting – circle of female acquaintances would, I fear, scarce survive it.'

He handed over the piece of paper, which she placed carefully in her reticule.

'Remember – no scrapes,' he warned.

Even as he said it, he was assailed by doubts. But as Edward re-entered the bookroom at that moment and Anthea quickly glided away, there was no opportunity to recant.

CHAPTER IV

It had been a dull, grey day of drizzle interspersed with periods of heavier rain. Since nightfall, thick clouds had obscured the moon so that the darkness was almost impenetrable. A nearby church clock struck the hour of one, its sharp, metallic note accentuating the silence which enfolded the sleeping neighbourhood, giving it an eerie quality.

It made no impression on the only people abroad in that place at this unlikely hour, four men leading a horse and cart. They came stealthily, entering by a gate which they knew would have been left open for them, though it should have been locked. Two of them carried shuttered lanterns which they had made use of from time to time on their way, even though they could almost walk the ground blindfold, so frequently did they make this journey.

They halted the horse, a poor specimen that had only just escaped the knacker's yard, and noiselessly removed the tools of their trade from the cart. These consisted of two heavy spades, two steel hooks like grappling irons attached to long ropes, a voluminous sack and a large, thick sheet. They divided these among themselves for transporting, the men with the lanterns taking the easier burdens.

No word was spoken either then or when they trod across the uneven ground to their objective. One of the men moved back a shutter from his lantern to light the way. The thin gleam briefly illumined the stones which they passed; some still upright, many leaning over at a crazy angle, with inscriptions long since worn away.

They halted presently beside a plot of freshly turned earth that had no stone upon it. One of the men grunted a command for more light. The shutters were removed from both lanterns, which were then set down at either end of the plot. They spread out the large sheet on the ground beside it, quietly depositing their tools upon this.

One of the group produced a bottle from his pocket, uncorked it, and took a long pull before passing it round to the others.

Having refreshed themselves sufficiently for the moment, they spat on their hands, picked up the spades, and began rapidly to shovel the earth from the plot on to their outspread sheet.

For some time they worked without speaking save for the occasional labouring grunt, until suddenly the spades encountered something solid. Apparently this happened sooner than had been anticipated, for one of the men was betrayed into a surprised comment.

'Shoved 'im in 'asty like,' he muttered.

There were grunts of agreement as the light revealed a wooden box under the thin layer of soil yet remaining.

One man jumped into the hole they had uncovered, while the others passed the steel hooks down to him, holding on to the ends of the attached ropes. Quickly and expertly – all their movements were those of individuals well practised in this gruesome exercise – he placed the hooks under the lid of the box. The others heaved on the ropes, and the lid yielded with a loud crack. He tossed it aside.

The sight must have struck terror into the heart of any ordinary mortal. But these men were hardened to the grisly business which they followed; indeed, it was nothing for them to repeat the performance several times in a night.

They hauled the dreadful bundle roughly to the surface, hastily stripping off the shroud and pushing the lifeless form it contained into the sack they had brought for the purpose. Having secured the top of the sack with rope, they heaved it to one side while they concentrated all their energies on replacing the earth from the sheet to the open grave, so that no sign would be evident next day that it had been disturbed. But first they tossed the shroud back into the empty coffin; for, ironically enough, stealing a shroud was a hanging matter, judged more serious than the snatching of a dead body.

Soon all was finished to their satisfaction. Once more the bottle was produced and did its rounds; then they hauled the sack with its horrific contents over to the waiting cart and tossed it unceremoniously inside. Next they placed the tools beside it; but this was done carefully, so that no injury from a sharp edge should be caused to their valuable haul. The surgeons paid well, but not for damaged goods.

They led the horse and cart through dark, malodorous alleys and byways until they came to the United Borough hospitals of Guy's and St Thomas's. They knew just whom to approach with their grisly merchandise.

The transaction completed, they disappeared into the night, leaving the hospital porter to convey the sack to the dissecting room of Mr Astley Cooper.

Astley Cooper was one of the most gifted former pupils of the renowned John Hunter, and had already made a name for himself in surgery. As lecturer in Anatomy at St Thomas's and surgeon at Guy's, he occupied the two most important posts in the United Borough hospitals. He held firmly to the view that dissection was essential in the study of anatomy, and had been known to declare that if a surgeon had not first operated on the dead, he could only mangle the living.

The law permitted the use of the bodies of executed criminals for dissection; but numbers available were not nearly sufficient to supply the needs of medical students. This situation had led to a callous trade in bodysnatching by creatures who came to be known as "resurrection men". Astley Cooper's attitude towards their activities was ambivalent. He despised the individuals who performed these ghoulish tasks, while recognising the unfortunate necessity of trading with them for surgical specimens.

He frequently stayed at the hospital late into the night. He came at once to the dissecting room when the porter summoned him. Dismissing the man – who went readily enough, having no taste for what was to follow – Astley Cooper adjusted the position of the candles in order to look more closely at the corpse lying on the table.

He was a little surprised to see at once that this was the body of a well nourished man. Most specimens brought in by the bodysnatchers were undersized and had obviously been poorly fed; the graves of poor people were more accessible to the bodysnatchers than those of the wealthier classes.

Before proceeding to an examination of the body, he glanced briefly at the face.

He froze in his tracks and looked again. Then he lifted a candle to study the features intently.

'Good God!' he exclaimed. 'Jermyn! Now what the devil – ah!'

His eyes travelled lower, coming to rest upon the dead man's chest. His fingers explored the area just above the heart, where a bullet hole appeared.

'Good God!' he muttered again.

Then he sighed, half in exasperation. It was unfortunate

that he should have been brought the corpse of a man who was well known to him, if not well liked. It was even more unfortunate that this would undoubtedly be a case for Bow Street.

'This investigation must be pursued,' declared Sir Nathaniel Conant, chief magistrate at Bow Street, 'with the utmost rigour.'

'Naturally, sir,' replied Runner Joseph Watts, standing stiffly to attention in his former military style.

'A member of the Quality – a friend of His Royal Highness the Prince Regent himself – to be foully murdered, then cast into a pauper's grave for his body to suffer the final monstrous indignity of being disturbed by those unnatural beings we term "resurrection men", and to end upon a dissecting table! It is beyond anything vile, and shall not go unpunished!'

'Not if I know it,' promised Watts, grimly. 'Have we anything to go upon in the case, sir?'

Sir Nathaniel pursed up his mouth. 'Precious little, so far, but I rely upon you to remedy that. I would put Townsend on to it, but that he's accompanied the Prince Regent to Longleat.'

Joseph Watts contented himself with a nod. John Townsend was a senior Bow Street Runner, one of two whose duty it was to protect the Royal Court.

'The facts are these,' continued the magistrate. 'Mr Astley Cooper, as medical consultant to the Jermyn family, undertook the melancholy task of informing the widow that her husband's murdered body had been discovered last night. How he contrived it, I know not, but the lady was not made aware of – hm! – the precise circumstances. Bear this in mind should you need to interview the family yourself. Lady Jermyn then informed Mr Astley Cooper that her husband had in fact been missing from home since last Monday, but that she had been unwilling to spread the news abroad. I will give you a résumé of the few facts he elicited from her.'

Watts listened attentively during this brief recital.

'There is one matter of interest,' concluded Sir Nathaniel. 'It seems that Lady Jermyn, though reluctant to appeal to us for help in finding her missing spouse, had requested the assistance of a gentleman not unknown to us. I mean, of course – '

'Captain Rutherford!' exclaimed Watts, in tones of satisfaction. 'Though he don't use the rank now that his Army days are over. Ah, he was a rattling good officer to work for, was the Captain, and he and I tackled some tricky business in our time. Intelligence Officer for the Duke, he was, sir, in them days.'

'Quite,' replied Sir Nathaniel, in slightly repressive tones. 'Well, you're a Bow Street Runner now, and doubtless your former military experience comes in useful. But the Honourable Justin Rutherford, to give him his proper, peace time title, may perhaps care to continue to work with us on the investigation of this case. If so, I don't scruple to tell you that his assistance should not be shunned. Indeed, I would welcome it, seeing that here, as in the former investigation, we are dealing with the Quality – tricky, very tricky, Watts. And the murdered man was an intimate associate of His Royal Highness.' He shook his head portentously.

'Yessir. So perhaps I should present myself at the Captain's – I should say, at Mr Rutherford's – quarters and see what he has to say about this affair?'

Sir Nathaniel nodded.

'I don't think you could do better,' he agreed.

This interview with his superior officer took place on Saturday morning; but it was late afternoon before Watts found Justin Rutherford at home. Although Selby, gentleman's gentleman to Justin, would normally have refused outright to discuss his master's comings and goings with an individual such as Watts, recent experience had taught him that the Runner was a privileged person in his employer's view, never to be denied access. He therefore informed Watts that he might hope to find Mr Rutherford at home between four and six o'clock.

The Runner did not waste any time, but employed the interval in seeking an interview with the porter at Guy's hospital. This individual was reluctant in the extreme to divulge the source of his supply of what he termed 'surgeons' necessities'; but Watts finally forced out of him an admission that it was some of the Borough gang.

'Their names,' rasped Watts.

But this was going too far for the porter. He took a firm stand on ignorance, and nothing the Runner said could move him from this position. As Watts was well aware of the equivocal situation, he knew that he could look for no support from Astley Cooper, so decided to obtain his information elsewhere.

He returned to Albemarle Street to find that Mr Rutherford was at home and willing to see him.

'Come to clap me up in Newgate, eh, Joe?' Justin greeted his former associate.

'Not this time, sir. Need your assistance – leastways, we're both on the same lay, so I've heard.'

Justin cocked an eyebrow, and motioned him to a seat. 'Hmm. Jermyn?'

'The same,' nodded Watts. 'He's turned up, guv. Murdered – shot.'

'The devil he has! Suppose you tell me the whole? Do the family know?'

Watts nodded again, and proceeded to explain matters.

'Unpleasant,' commented Justin wryly, at the end of the

Runner's account. 'I wonder how he came to be buried without benefit of clergy?'

'That's the way it must've been, sir. Someone shot him, bunged him into a coffin, and put him underground. The Borough boys wouldn't have had a hand in any o' that – they dig corpses out, not bury 'em. Not to say the grave-digger at that cemetery mightn't know something – bound to, come to think of it.'

'Yes, I believe we must have a word with him. Do you know which graveyard it is? But I suppose not, since you could get nothing out of the porter at Guy's. These Borough boys, now – any way you can lay hands on 'em?'

'I've a notion who some of 'em are, and I know for a fact they frequent the flash houses around those parts, sir. I'll look in at one or two, see what I can uncover.'

'We'll look in together, I think, Joe. You might be glad of an ally. Oh, never fear, I can rough myself up a trifle – I promise you won't recognise me yourself when I've done. When's the best time to catch these birds?'

'Early evening, I reckon, sir, before things get too lively. But you don't need to come, as I can easy enough get another Runner, seeing as this is a murder job.'

'Surely you can't intend to deprive me of the chance of seeing a bit of low life?' demanded Justin, with a grin.

'Low life is right, sir. They're a mortal ugly lot, in the flash houses.'

'No uglier, I dare say, than one finds at prizefights or a cocking, not to mention our little skirmishes together in the Peninsula, what?'

Watts gave a reminiscent grin. 'Not saying you bain't up to snuff, sir,' he conceded.

'Good of you. There's one other pointer we've got, by the way.'

He proceeded to tell Watts of Anthea's revelations.

'So far, that seems to be the last time Jermyn was seen

alive. I think we must interview this modiste. Perhaps it would be best to go there first, while I still present a reasonably creditable appearance. It may be, Joe, that this will turn out to be a devilish sordid affair at the end of it – but, damme, one finds it hard to resist trying to solve a mystery!'

CHAPTER V

'Close the shutters, Miss Parker,' commanded Madame Yvonne. 'We shall do no more business tonight.'

'Yes, Madame,' replied her chief assistant, a thin, not to say scrawny female, with a facial expression of bored superiority rather like that of a camel. 'Shall I dimiss the others?'

'Yes, but tell Miles and Smith to take their work home and return with it finished on Monday. We cannot afford to fall behind with Lady Deanesford's order for her daughter's trousseau. And if there should be *one* finger-mark – but I don't need to tell you that, I fancy.'

'No, indeed, Madame,' assented Miss Parker, who had worked her way up in the business, and knew almost as much about it as Madame herself. 'I am not perfectly satisfied with Fuller. She set her stitches very ill in the last hour of work yesterday evening – said the candles were guttering.'

'Then get rid of her. There's no shortage of seam-stresses, I believe, who won't think to complain about the lighting arrangements in the basement. That will be all.'

'Yes, Madame.'

Miss Parker hurred away belowstairs to dismiss her minions, while her employer cast a quick look around the showroom to see that all was in order before moving towards the front door to secure the lock.

When she reached it, she saw two men standing on the threshold about to enter.

She gave them a quick, assessing glance. One of them was undoubtedly a gentleman; the other appeared to be a groom, or some other outdoor servant.

'Madame Yvonne, I believe?' said the gentleman in easy tones. 'May we come in for a moment? We wish to talk to you.'

Before she could either give or withhold consent, they had stepped inside, closing the door behind them.

'I was about to close the premises,' she said coldly.

'Then by all means do so, ma'am,' returned the gentleman, cordially. 'I dare say you work shockingly long hours, as it is. Far be it from us to extend them. The favour of a few minutes of your time is all we require.'

She hesitated, then locked and bolted the door. Neither of them had the look of a felon; indeed, there was something quite otherwise even about the man she had taken for a groom. He had the manner of some kind of official, she now thought.

'As you say, my time is limited,' she agreed, in the same frigid tone. 'What is your business here?'

She did not invite them to sit, so all three were standing in a group near the door.

'Perhaps I should first make myself known to you, ma'am,' began Justin. 'My name is Rutherford and my companion is Mr Watts.'

He bowed briefly as he spoke, and Watts had already removed his hat. Madame replied with a curt nod.

The name told her at once that she was dealing with a male member of Viscount Rutherford's family, but she was puzzled to account for his presence in her salon. All the same, tact was necessary.

'Perhaps you had better be seated for a moment,' she said grudgingly, waving them to a group of the cramped, though elegant, green and gold chairs. 'I must insist that I cannot stay longer.'

They sat down, Watts grimacing at the constriction of what he inwardly phrased putting a quart into a pint pot.

Justin nodded in acknowledgement.

'Quite so. We will come to the point at once. I believe Lady Jermyn is one of your clients, ma'am?'

A slight guard came over the modiste's far from open countenance. She nodded.

'The Lady's husband, Sir Aubrey Jermyn, was seen on your premises on Monday last, about quarter past two. Can you inform us at what time he left?'

She raised her eyebrows.

'Sir Aubrey Jermyn *here*! You are mistaken.'

'Not so,' he replied, in a firm tone. 'My authority is incontrovertible, I assure you.'

'Then who is it?'

He shook his head. 'I am not at liberty to reveal that, I fear.'

She stared at him for a moment as though she would force the information out of him by hypnosis. Seeing this had no effect, she flung out her hands in a gesture which showed Justin that she had some claim to a French name, if not to that of Yvonne.

'It is a nonsense! I myself was here on Monday last, all day, as I usually am, for one does not leave valued clients to underlings, you understand. And I saw nothing of this gentleman you mention. He was not here. Now will you please leave?'

'A moment, ma'am. Do you know Sir Aubrey?'

She shrugged. 'By sight, of course, as one is familiar with most members of the *ton*.'

'Not personally?'

'Such as I, sir?' she demanded, with a cynical sneer. 'We do not move in the same circles.'

'Then why was he seated in your private apartments, apparently awaiting someone?'

Justin snapped the words at her almost as a blow. If he hoped to catch her unawares, he was to be disappointed, however.

'He was not!' she snapped back. 'Your informant was mistaken, that's all! And now, if you'll excuse me, Mr Rutherford – '

She stood up, pointedly waiting for them to go.

Justin glanced at Watts, who had so far remained silent, then slowly rose. At that moment, Miss Parker came into the room.

She started to say that she had finished, but closed her lips upon the utterance on seeing the two visitors.

'Yes, yes, you may go,' said Madame, quickly.

'Just a moment, ma'am,' said Justin, gently, advancing towards the startled female. 'This is your assistant, I take it? Miss – er – '

'Parker. You can have nothing to say to her. Good night, Parker.'

'That's where you're wrong, ma'am,' said Watts, moving over to join Justin in front of the assistant. 'Now, see here, Miss Parker, there's just one or two questions we'd like you to answer. Nothing to be afraid of,' he added, kindly, seeing the woman's terrified look. 'Just you speak up and tell the truth, that's the dandy.'

'Tell the truth – of course she'll tell the truth! That's to say, *if* she were to answer your impertinent questions, which of course she don't intend to, seeing that you've no right to come here pestering people! Now remove yourselves at once, or I call the Law!'

'I *am* the Law,' said Watts, displaying his badge of office, the Runner's baton with a crown stamp on it. 'And if ye don't choose to answer me, maybe ye'll prefer to come along to Bow Street and answer the magistrate.'

Miss Parker gave a little scream, and her employer eyed her scornfully.

'Oh, sit down, you silly creature,' she said, contemptuously. 'All they want to know is if Sir Aubrey Jermyn was here on Monday last. I've already told them that he was *not*. You need only confirm it.'

'Diddled, b'God,' muttered Justin to Watts.

'Well, miss?' demanded Watts, coaxingly. 'Would you recognise that there gennelman if ye set eyes on him?'

Miss Parker gave a strangled assent.

'Now I want you to think *v-ery* carefully,' went on Watts, in a warning tone. 'Remember as it's an offence to give false information to a law officer. Did you or did you not see this gennelman Jermyn anywhere on these premises last Monday?'

Miss Parker had evidently made a strong effort to pull herself together, for she now looked more like a camel than ever. She glanced at her employer before answering, then came out with a decided negative.

'I trust you're satisfied,' said Madame Yvonne, in acid tones. 'Now will you go?'

'We would like first to take a look around the premises,' said Justin.

She gave him a withering glance. 'I'm not at all sure what *your* part is in this affair, but I must state at once that until a warrant is produced for a search, I refuse utterly to allow any such thing. And since I myself am unaware of what I stand accused, I think it unlikely that you'll obtain a warrant.'

'We're investigating a case of murder,' Watts informed her. 'Murder of the man Jermyn.'

She took this as calmly as she had accepted everything throughout; but Parker went into strong hysterics. Madame slapped her face.

When the turmoil had died down and Parker was

reduced to a quietly sobbing heap in her chair, Watts returned to the attack.

'According to our information, the deceased was last seen alive on your premises on Monday afternoon. You say ye never set eyes on him – mebbe not, but someone must've done. We'll need to question all your employees and take a look at the premises.'

'This is outrageous!' declared Madame. 'Because some unknown person states that this unfortunate gentleman was here, am I to be treated like a criminal? Is this English justice?'

'We haven't yet come to the courts, ma'am,' put in Justin, gently. 'If I might suggest that you should co-operate with the Runner? Are your staff still here, or have they departed?'

'Parker has dismissed them until Monday,' she said, in grudging tones.

Watts took out his notebook.

'Then I'll need their names and to know where they can be found, if you please.'

Evidently Madame felt it was desirable to comply with Mr Rutherford's suggestion, for she supplied the necessary information. Only five members of the staff besides Miss Parker worked in the building, one in the showroom and four in the basement. Two men who moved heavy goods and drove the firm's vehicle worked outside, in the mews.

When the necessary details were entered in the Runner's notebook, Justin looked enquiringly at Madame, indicating with a gesture that she should conduct them around the building. After another bitter protest to which they paid no heed, she capitulated and led the way.

At the rear of the salon on the left-hand side were several small curtained closets used as fitting rooms. She swept aside the curtain from one of these, indicating that all were similar. A short passage ran between the closets and what appeared to be a large room on the right, with neither door nor window giving on to the showroom. A few steps along the passage, however, brought them to a door.

'May we enter?' asked Justin, a hand on the doorknob.

She shrugged. 'It's only our storeroom and finishing workroom, but enter if you insist.'

They opened the door and looked inside.

The room was fitted with shelves on which were several lengths of cloth. A couple of dressmakers' stands, a trestle table and two large trunks stood on the floor. Viewing it critically, Justin decided that the room was smaller than he would have expected, to judge from the length of the wall which divided it off from the showroom.

He mentioned the fact. 'Is there not another room adjoining this one?'

'Yes, there is indeed!' snapped Madame. 'But that is a private sitting room for my own use, and nothing whatever to do with the business premises! It cannot concern you in the slightest!'

'Since it's a private sitting room,' replied Justin, equably, 'that will be why there's no communicating door leading from this room. But presumably there does exist an entrance to it somewhere?'

'Of course. There is a door to it in the main passage which runs the length of the building from my private entrance in the side street.'

'And this passage leads into the main one?'

She nodded curtly.

'There is no other access to the sitting room but by way of the door in the main passage?' he insisted.

'No.'

He walked back into the showroom again, closely followed by the others, and gazed consideringly at the blank outer wall of the two rooms. At the extreme end on the right was what appeared to be a tall, narrow cupboard. He approached it.

'This, for instance, doesn't lead into it?'

'Certainly not! It's merely a small closet. You may see for yourself, since your curiosity seems to know no bounds.'

She pushed open the door in a casual way, evidently intending to close it again quickly. But Justin stepped inside, subjecting the small room to a keen scrutiny. It had no furnishings, apart from a small mirror on the wall. His quick eye soon detected the hidden door on the left-hand wall as described by Anthea, but he gave no sign.

'As you say, ma'am.'

He retreated, and she closed the door with a snap.

'May we now see the private room, please?'

'This is an imposition!' she stormed. 'I dare say you'll be wanting to view my bedchamber next! I can see no justification for it whatever, and have a good mind to lodge a complaint at Bow Street!'

'Do so, ma'am,' invited Watts, coolly. 'But I doubt it'll be well received. This is a murder inquiry, and the victim last seen alive here. No more nonsense, *if* ye please, ma'am.'

She looked as if she would argue once more, but changed her mind, shutting her lips in rat trap style. In silence she led the way along the short passage where they were standing, into a much wider one.

Here she turned to the right. Glancing left, Justin and Watts saw a street door with a fanlight over it at that end of the passage. Evidently this was Madame's private entrance from the side street. A staircase was close by, ascending to the upper storey.

Directly opposite the junction of the two passages was

another flight of stairs, this time leading down to the basement, and uncarpeted.

The proprietress gestured impatiently that they should follow her. A few yards along the passage they reached a door which she proceeded to unlock with a key she produced from a pocket of her gown.

'My sitting room, gentlemen,' she said mockingly, standing aside for them to enter. 'And much like any other, if I mistake not.'

Justin and Watts walked into the room and studied it in silence. It was precisely as Anthea had described it; and, knowing where to look, Justin had no difficulty in detecting the second, inner secret door.

He neither approached this, nor made any mention of it.

He glanced up at the only window in the room, set high in the wall beside the door, and reflected that no one could possibly look through it into the room without using a ladder to do so.

Satisfied, he nodded at Watts.

'Thank you, ma'am, you've been most accommodating,' he said smoothly. 'And now, if we might just trouble you to conduct us downstairs to the basement?'

'This is outrageous!' she exploded. 'What possible interest can my workroom downstairs hold for you?'

'We'll be the judge o' that,' answered Watts sternly.

She shrugged and led the way down the stone steps. There was nothing remarkable about the workroom excepting the poor light in which its unfortunate occupants were obliged to pursue their tasks. A corridor beside it, also dim, led to the cobbled yard where the pump and privy were situated. A door on the left-hand wall gave access to the mews; Madame's stabling was here, together with that of several neighbouring shopkeepers.

'Interesting,' commented Justin, as they took their way

homewards. 'Jermyn could easily enough enter and leave that private room by Madame's street door without attracting undue attention. Busy enough for no one to notice.'

Watts nodded. 'Yes, and not too difficult to sneak in or out the back way. Workmen busy in the stables, or out on deliveries, and the light's so poor anyone could slip past the workroom with those poor molls bent over their needlework. So the lady pops in unseen through the cupboard, while the gent does likewise by another route. Don't tell us aught about the murder, though, do it, sir? Expect the culprit's the lady's husband – powerful motive, if he found out about their goings-on. But when did it happen, and where? And who pops the corpse into a coffin and buries it, eh? 'Course, it's easy to see why Madame there – ' he jerked his head backwards to indicate the gown shop – 'don't want to admit nothing. She didn't see the gennelman, I don't think! Lose a good customer, she might, if she admits to agreeing to an assignation between the two, leave alone the harm any scandal would do to her business.'

'True – she was quick to warn her assistant to say nothing. What puzzles me, though, Joe, is why no one seems to have set eyes on Jermyn after he left his house on Monday, until my niece did so. You'd best set someone on to question the crossing sweepers and hackney drivers in the vicinity of his house and hereabouts. What was he doing before he kept his appointment with the unknown lady? And when did he leave Madame Yvonne's premises to go to his death?'

CHAPTER VI

The news of Jermyn's murder soon spread, though the exact circumstances of the discovery of the body were kept secret. The affair was exclaimed over in the clubs and spoken of in hushed whispers in the drawing rooms. The story ran that his body had been discovered in the vicinity of Guy's hospital and carried in for medical attention, but too late, alas. There was a bullet wound through the heart which must, according to the renowned Dr Astley Cooper, have killed him instantly.

Speculation produced a number of possibilities, but no one seemed satisfied with any of them.

'Could be footpads,' suggested Davenport, one of Jermyn's particular circle. 'Not that I ever heard of one taking to firearms. What those gentry try for is a quick, crippling blow with a cudgel or a weighted length of canvas to stun their victim for long enough to relieve him of his blunt and jewellery. Damme if Spendlove didn't fall foul of a pair of 'em last month in Bruton Street, of all places! Don't ask me what the watch was doing – we all know the Charleys are useless – and the Foot patrol had gone off duty, as they do around midnight.'

The Honourable Nigel Ambrose shook his head over this.

'Couldn't have been a duel?' someone else suggested, dubiously.

'Out of fashion, my dear fellow,' scoffed Ambrose. Besides, what about the seconds? Deuced rum affair, if not only the principal in a duel took to his heels in fright when he saw he'd killed his man, but the seconds as well! Besides, there'd be a medico standing by – deuced bad *ton* to have an affair of honour without one, as any of the old school would tell you. And then again, who'd appoint a meeting in the neighbourhood of Guy's hospital, I ask you? No, seems to me that poor old Aubrey must have had an enemy somewhere who was fanatical enough to take a pot shot at him.'

'Wouldn't be surprising,' responded Davenport. '*De mortuis* and all that, but there were those who felt less than friendly towards him, and with some justification, one must allow. A few husbands, for instance – no need of names.'

The others nodded.

'Especially not since Drewe's coming this way,' warned one of them. 'Letitia Drewe and Jermyn were like two turtle doves not so long since, what?'

'All over for some months,' said Davenport, in a low tone. 'They made no secret of the affaire. It was the same with most of Jermyn's inamoratas. I rather think, though, there was someone lately whom he wished to keep dark. D'you know anything, Ambrose? You two were always thick as thieves.'

Ambrose shook his head and turned to greet the Honourable Peter Drewe, a somewhat vacuous man in his late thirties already developing a paunch. The talk was tactfully steered on to sporting topics, in which everyone took some interest, if only financial. Sure enough, eventually yet another wager was being recorded in the betting book

'Me pore old feet,' complained Watts, sinking into the

chair which Justin thoughtfully pushed forward for him, 'are fair killin' me, give you m'word, Captain!'

'Been on the hoof all the forenoon, have you?' asked Justin sympathetically. 'Well, I've no remedy for sore feet, but I can supply a soothing draught for irritation of the nerves. What'll it be, Joe?'

'A tankard of home brewed wouldn't come amiss, sir, thanking you kindly.'

This was supplied; and Watts, having downed half of it at a gulp, began to give details of his recent researches with occasional reference to his notebook.

'Start with the most important, sir. I found a jarvey who remembers taking our man to the shop in Bond Street in his hackney at about two o'clock on Monday. Picked him up at a house in St James's Square, and knows which one, on account of he was summoned by a footman to the door. Said he remembered that fare particular, as when he set him down at the side entrance to the shop, he was instructed to go back there at four sharp to pick the cove up again. Which he did, but never sight nor sound of him, even though the jarvey hung about for close on half an hour. Slung his hook then, he says, and I can't blame him.'

'Did he not knock on the door?'

Watts nodded. 'Twice, but no one answered, so he went back to his vehicle and waited. Then another fare came along.'

'Hmm. So Jermyn failed to appear at the appointed time,' Justin mused. 'I take it you checked the jarvey's statement? But of course you did,' he added hastily, seeing the pained look on the Runner's face. 'Two possibilities there, then, wouldn't you say? Either Jermyn decided for some reason to leave by another way, or – '

'Or he never left at all.' finished Watts, grimly. 'And that would mean he was murdered on Madame's premises, most like, indoors or outside. Of course, he *could* possibly have been abducted. And that brings me to the rest of my report, sir, regarding the workpeople at the shop.'

'One moment.' Jermyn raised a hand to halt the Runner. 'The house in St James's Square from which Jermyn took a hackney – did you chance to discover who resides there?'

'I did. It's my Lord Escott.'

'Escott – the man Jermyn favoured as a husband for his niece. Well, naturally they would be close friends, one supposes. I wonder how long Jermyn had been with Escott before leaving for Madame Yvonne's salon? Seems to me that might possibly tell us something. I'll undertake that part of the inquiry, Joe.'

'Do you know the gennelman, sir?'

'Not to say know him – know of him. Think I've met him once or twice, but he's another generation, y'know. Not much in my style, moreover.' He broke off, frowning. 'What's the remainder, Joe? Did you interview the work-people at Yvonne's?'

'Yessir. Five females beside that Miss Parker, and the two men in the yard. I'll run through the statements quick as I can, for I reckon only two of 'em's any use to us. Girl called Mary Baines works in the salon, helping Miss Parker. She recalls bein' in trouble Monday, on account of having shown a customer into a cupboard instead of a fitting room. Had warning about that – any more mistakes and it's the sack.'

'My niece Anthea,' nodded Justin. 'Why should she have made that particular mistake, I wonder? There are a number of other fitting rooms. Surely they couldn't all have been occupied?'

'Reckon there was something more there, but she clammed up, sir. Couldn't get it out o' her nowise. Might have been warned to say nothing – she wasn't the only one, neither.'

'Indeed? I'd hoped that as you saw them on a Sunday when they were all in their own homes and away from Madame's possible intervention, that you'd have caught 'em unaware, so to speak. But pray continue, Joe.'

'Three of the females employed as seamstresses – names, Miles, Smith and Fuller – reckon they heard nothing, saw nothing nor don't want to know nothing. The fourth, though, Bates, is a horse o' a different colour.'

'Oh?'

Watts nodded. 'Cocky, but scared with it. She'd a follower visiting her, name of Carter – danged if I know where I've clapped eyes on him afore, but I'll take my oath that I have. It struck me he wasn't best pleased to see me, neither, when he learnt my trade. No matter, it'll come to me. Any road, this female Bates hinted she'd a tale or two to tell of Madame if she chose. Of course, I pressed hard for details, as you may suppose, sir, but there's no doing aught with females when they prim up their mouths and sit tight short of beatin' 'em, which bain't in my line. This cove of hers says he works for a saddler in the Borough High Street. I've not had time yet to go along and see, but I will, never fear. Something smoky about the pair of 'em, if you ask me. Seemingly they're to be wed when they can find enough blunt.'

'What of the two men in the yard? Did they chance to see Jermyn leaving by that way out?'

'Thick as two sticks, sir, and they were absent part of the time collecting goods. I'm satisfied they didn't see him, though.'

'We need to interrogate that gravedigger, Joe, once we've ascertained which is the burial ground concerned. I think our next move must be to pay a visit to those flash houses of yours and try to trace the resurrection men. But first I'll call upon my Lord Escott.'

After a short wait in a cool, chequer-board tiled hall surrounded by marble pillars, Justin was informed by a liveried footman that my lord was at home in the social as well as the physical sense. Accordingly, the visitor was led upstairs to the drawing room, decorated in modern style with pale blue plaster walls topped by a frieze, and with a plaster medallion enclosing a pair of classical figures over the fireplace.

Lord Escott came forward to greet him. He was a man in his sixties, distinguished looking, with iron grey hair and a thin, waspish countenance. He raised his rather sparse eyebrows sardonically as he made his bow. 'An unlooked for pleasure, Mr Rutherford. Pray be seated. Can I offer you any refreshment?'

'Nothing, I thank you. It's good of you to see me – I promise not to take up too much of your time.'

Justin's tone was easy, but his feelings did not match it. He scarcely knew this man, so it would be difficult to find a suitable approach to the business in hand. They both sat down.

'Time is something of which I have sufficient at present,' replied Escott, in bland tones. 'But since you undertake to occupy but little of it, I collect that you wish to see me on a matter of business? I cannot conceive what it may be. Pray enlighten me.'

'A matter of grim business, I fear,' returned Justin. 'The death of Sir Aubrey Jermyn.'

He watched the other man intently as he said this, but saw no sign in his face of any other emotion than slight boredom.

'Ah, yes. A sad affair – and a mysterious one. I trust it does not concern you too closely? He was not, I believe, an intimate friend of your family?'

'No. But I collect that he was of yourself.'

'Oh, yes. I've known Jermyn for – dear me, one doesn't care to recall how many years. But may I ask – ' he waved a deprecating hand, but his lips sneered – 'why we are speaking on such a melancholy subject, Mr Rutherford? *You* cannot have a personal interest in the matter, since you acknowledge that poor Jermyn was not a friend.'

'Not a personal interest, true. I am acting on Lady Jermyn's instigation. Before news of his death was conveyed to her, she had requested me to try and find him. You may know that he had been missing from home during the past week.'

'One had heard something, of course, in the clubs. But surely, Mr Rutherford, now that the unfortunate Jermyn has been – er – found – ' he paused to survey Justin with a sneer – 'your good office can be considered as having been discharged, and you need no longer concern yourself in what must, I am sure, be a tedious matter?'

This was so patently true that Justin found himself a trifle at a disadvantage. He let no sign of this appear, however, but persevered.

'I take it you're acquainted with the facts, my lord? Jermyn was murdered – shot through the heart. There is still the matter of discovering his murderer.'

'I dare say it's stupid of me,' drawled Escott, half closing his eyes in a pained expression, 'but I did have the notion that the Crown made annual payments to the magistrates and officers at Bow Street to ensure that they should deal with matters of the kind. Do you mean to infer that these useful – if occasionally tiresome – services are no longer available, and that the Quality are now obliged to shift for themselves? Upon my oath – ' shaking his head sadly – 'I don't know what the country's coming to, sir.'

'To be plain with you, Lord Escott, I'm giving a helping

hand to the chief magistrate at Bow Street, Sir Nathaniel Conant, as a matter of choice,' replied Justin, in downright tones. He was somewhat nettled by the other's deliberately insulting manner. 'I think you might assist the investigation, if you chose. For instance, Jermyn was with you on the Monday morning of his disappearance. Did he mention anything to you which might throw some light on that?'

'So I am to be – what is the correct term? – interrogated,' said Escott, with an unpleasant smile. 'Dear me, what strange tastes you possess, my dear fellow – and I always heard that you were by way of being an antiquarian. Still, I suppose there can be no harm in humouring you,' he added, as his visitor made an impatient movement. 'No, I cannot recall any mention being made of a withdrawal from society. Indeed, it's vastly difficult to recollect the details of a trivial conversation of more than a week ago.'

He smothered a yawn ostentatiously.

'And he made no mention of where he would be going after leaving you?' persisted Justin.

'Really, I begin to find this prodigiously tiresome, Mr Rutherford. May I remind you that I'm in no way obliged to answer your – I fear there is no other word for it – impertinent queries?'

Justin's face hardened. 'A man has been done to death, moreover a man whom you admit was an intimate friend. Surely you would wish to give any assistance possible to those who seek his murderer?'

'I admit that I've know Jermyn for a good many years, but as to his being an intimate friend – ' he pursed up his thin lips.

'I understand that he was promoting a union between yourself and his ward, nevertheless.'

'Ah, yes,' said Escott, softly.

'That argues a degree of intimacy, one would think.'

'Very well, I concede the hypothesis. But I do not believe I can help you. I have very little recollection of our conversation that morning.'

'He did not say, for instance, that he intended to visit the premises of a fashionable modiste in Bond Street during the afternoon?'

Escott raised his eyebrows mockingly. 'You think he was contemplating a masquerade in female attire? It's an interesting notion, certainly.'

Justin rose to his feet impatiently. 'You must be an expert fencer, my lord! I'll tell you in plain terms that Jermyn was observed in a private room at the premises of Madame Yvonne that same afternoon, and was never seen alive afterwards. Now will you be pleased to remember anything he may have said of his reason for that visit?'

'May I remind you that you have no authority in this matter, and that I don't care for your tone?'

Justin nodded. 'You're in the right of it. I was relying – perhaps mistakenly – on enlisting your goodwill. It seems I've unwittingly forfeited that, so there's no purpose in prolonging this interview. I wish you good day, my lord.'

He bowed stiffly, and turned toward the door, but Escott put up a hand to detain him.

'One moment. There's one piece of information I can offer you as a sop to your injured sensibilities. It is that the modiste Madame Yvonne – I collect that is her name nowadays – has, like myself, known Jermyn for a very long time.'

Justin halted, directing a keen glance at Escott.

'Indeed? You would say she is his mistress?'

Escott shook his head. 'No, not at present. That is ancient history. But there was a time, in Brighton – however, you should ask Madame herself. I've no desire to enact the role of tale-bearer.'

'It would save valuable time if you would tell me the whole,' said Justin. 'We – the Bow Street Runner conducting the investigation and myself – have already interviewed the modiste, and she denies categorically that Jermyn was ever on her premises. We had no better success with her workpeople, either, who had evidently been primed to tell the same story. Yet I have positive information from a totally reliable source that he was seen there at about a quarter past two o'clock on Monday.'

'Ah, was he so?' Escott smiled unpleasantly. 'You don't surprise me, my dear Rutherford. But with the best will in the world, I fear I must disappoint you in the matter of providing you with a full account of Jermyn's past. I know only what he has let slip from time to time. The rest is rumour and gossip. One thing I do think you may rest assured of, however. Whatever their relations in the past, Jermyn and the female Yvonne were strictly on business terms nowadays. As to what that business may have been – ' He broke off and shrugged.

Seeing that there was nothing further to be learned from the man at present, Justin took his leave. He had managed to keep his temper in check during the interview, but now he strode out rapidly to work off his disgust. He had known Escott by reputation as a hardened roué and a man of little or no scruple; coming face to face with him had not improved this image. That such a man should have been considered as a fit husband for Miss Jermyn was an outrage, he thought hotly. There was one benefit to her from her uncle's death, at any rate; no one now could force such a vile match upon her.

The thought of her soon banished his black mood.

CHAPTER VII

'I don't scruple to admit to you, Anthea,' said Charlotte Jermyn, tossing back her yellow curls with an impatient gesture, 'that I cannot *truly* grieve over my uncle's death. The manner of it, yes, for murder is horrible, and no one could be other than profoundly shocked. But it would be hypocritical of me to pretend that I feel the deep sorrow that a niece might be expected to experience in like circumstances. My only true sorrow is for my poor aunt, who, naturally enough, feels dreadfully at present.'

She glanced apologetically at Justin as she finished speaking. He had accompanied Anthea to the Jermyns' house on a visit of condolence, but it did not surprise him to learn that there was no need of condolences as far as Miss Jermyn was concerned. Lady Jermyn, of course, was not at present receiving visitors.

'I am sorry to say what may shock you, Mr Rutherford,' she continued, 'although I fancy I made my attitude towards my uncle sufficiently plain to you when last we met. He never cared for me, and indifference begets indifference. I fear I am not the kind of female who can simulate feelings for propriety's sake – I prefer plain dealing.'

'Pray don't concern yourself on that head, Miss Jermyn. My long association with Anthea has rendered me almost completely unshockable, I assure you,' he replied, with a quizzical look towards his niece, who grimaced at him.

'Besides, I prefer plain dealing myself. That being so, I'd like you to know that it's my intention to pursue the investigation into your uncle's murder together with the Bow Street Runner who's been assigned to the case. That is, of course, with Lady Jermyn's permission. May I count on your support in obtaining this? I think it may be to the family's advantage to allow me to act as a buffer, so to speak, between yourselves and officialdom.'

She nodded. 'Indeed, I am sure Aunt Amelia would prefer you to continue to help us, sir. It will be more comfortable for us to answer any questions there may be to you, rather than the Bow Street officers. But perhaps there is very little more you need to learn from us?'

He glanced at her appreciatively before replying. The conventional black she was wearing suited her fair colouring to admiration, making her blonde curls look even brighter. Her very blue eyes met his in an enquiring look which for some reason he found provocative. It was that pert little nose that did it, he reflected with a smile.

'On the contrary, ma'am, with your indulgence there are one or two queries I should like to put to you now. It's quite likely, too, that I may find it necessary to call upon you from time to time with further applications for your assistance.'

He caught Anthea's satirical eye as he said this, and looked hastily away.

'By all means, Mr Rutherford. And since I wish to spare my aunt's feelings as much as possible, pray address to me any questions you may need to ask of her. I can obtain the answers for you, if need be. But what is it you wish to know at present?'

He gave a little bow. 'You're very good, Miss Jermyn. The first point on which I hope you can help me concerns the modiste, Madame Yvonne. I collect that she is patronised by most ladies of the *ton*. Can you tell me how long your aunt has been a client?'

'Madame Yvonne?' repeated Charlotte, obviously puzzled. 'Oh, for ever, I should think! At least – ' realising that this answer was scarcely any help – 'for as long as she has been in Bond Street.'

'And how long would that be? Or don't you know, since most likely it goes back to your schooldays?' he said, smiling at her in what Anthea thought of as a very oncoming way.

'I can't be sure,' she said, looking down in slight confusion. 'But I do recall Aunt Amelia saying my uncle had particularly asked her to patronise Madame when she first set up in Bond Street, and not only that, but to recommend her to friends. Aunt says she thought it so odd of him, and I think at the time perhaps she did just wonder – ' She broke off.

'But just as you say,' she continued, 'I didn't learn this from my aunt until recently, because I was far too young at the time it occurred. I can't quite think why she should have spoken of it to me – ' she wrinkled her brow in a way that Justin found most fetching – 'but I suppose some chance remark may have reminded her of it.'

'Well, *I* can tell you how long the shop has been there,' supplied Anthea. 'Mama was talking about it after you left us on Saturday, and she said it was opened nine years ago, in 1807. Mama thinks that Yvonne originally came from France, but that she had another shop at first, in a humbler situation in London.'

'But I don't see – ' began Charlotte.

'Yes, why are you interested in Yvonne?' demanded the less inhibited Anthea. 'Oh, I believe I have the glimmering of a notion? You think there may have been some connection between her and Sir Aubrey Jermyn in the past, since she was permitting him to use her premises for assignations. And what Charlotte has just told you strengthens that notion, of course – '

'Assignations?' repeated Charlotte, puzzled.

'Oh, you don't know, of course,' said Anthea.

She and Charlotte were sitting side by side on a sofa, and she drew confidentially towards her friend.

'There are certain matters with which I must acquaint you, I see, but I'll spare your blushes, and not do so before Justin.'

She addressed herself to her amused relative.

'Kindly remove yourself. There's a bookcase over yonder where I'm sure you may find some improving work to enable you to pass the time agreeably until our confidences are done.'

Her dictatorial manner was rewarded by a suitable humble obedience. After a short interval of low toned, hurried conversation, he was once more summoned to her side.

'A word in your ear, good Uncle, and then my part as conspirator is done, and Charlotte will be ready to answer anything you ask of her.'

She rose, and quickly informed him in a low tone that she had said nothing to her friend of their suspicions regarding Lady St Clare. He nodded and resumed his seat, looking at Charlotte.

'One more question, ma'am, by your indulgence. Is your aunt at all acquainted with Viscountess St Clare?'

She looked puzzled at the change of ground.

'Why, yes, she has become so of late, though formerly we were only on nodding terms. But when we were last at Wynsfield, our country house, you know, the St Clares were visiting our neighbours there, Lord and Lady Glynder. My uncle and aunt have always been on most friendly terms with the Glynders, and so naturally we all came together a good deal at various social gatherings in the neighbourhood. After we returned to Town, the acquaintance was kept up to a certain extent, though I fancy my aunt – well, it did seem to me that my uncle –' She broke off, evidently embarrassed.

'Well, that is famous!' exclaimed Anthea, enthusiastically. 'Pray what is Lady St Clare's baptismal name, Charlotte?'

'Her *baptismal* name? What on earth can it signify?' demanded the puzzled girl. 'I can't think what you mean, Anthea!'

'Yes, yes, never mind what I mean! Pray tell me at once if you know it!'

'Dearest Anthea, if you have a fault,' reproved her friend gently, 'it is that you seek to drive everyone along at breakneck pace! Cannot you cure her of it, Mr Rutherford?'

He grinned ruefully. 'Surely you can't possibly have been in company with the two of us for as little as ten minutes without seeing that I have positively no influence over my niece? You should pity me, ma'am, rather than reprove me.'

'Reprove you? Oh, no!' she exclaimed in tones of mock outrage. 'I would not for the world take it upon myself – '

The look they exchanged of amusement with an undercurrent of strong attraction quite exasperated Anthea. She considered it ill-timed of Justin to pursue a flirtation at the precise moment when she hoped to learn something of great importance. Surely he, too, needed this information? She cut ruthlessly into their badinage.

'That's all very well, but I see what you will be at, Charlotte – you mean to tease me by making me wait for an answer. Wretched creature! But you need not trouble yourself – I'll find out by some other means.'

She turned a look of pique on them.

Charlotte laughed. 'I'm sorry, my love. I can't imagine why you should wish to know it, but Lady St Clare's first name is Stella.'

Anthea threw a triumphant glance at Justin.

'You wouldn't chance to have anything – say an invitation card, for instance – in her own handwriting? These things are usually printed, I know, and the names filled in by a secretary, or some such person,' she added, a shade despondently. 'But anything would do. Oh, of course! Your aunt will most likely have received a letter of condolence? Or if not yet, she'll certainly do so, and then you could show it to us.'

Charlotte shook her head. 'Well, yes, so she has. It was handed in by a footman this morning. It's not a personal letter, however, Anthea, but simply a black edged printed condolence card with the appropriate names written in the blank spaces. The degree of acquaintance was not such that a personal note was called for. You may certainly see it if you wish – I'll fetch it.'

She did so. Anthea scrutinised the card with Justin; but both shook their heads. The careful copperplate script was not at all like that on the note in Anthea's possession, and was almost certainly inscribed by an employee's hand.

'Upon my word,' exclaimed Charlotte, scrutinising their intent faces, 'I'm becoming prodigiously curious! What *is* all this about? Has it any connection with my uncle's – murder?'

'It may well have a connection,' replied Justin quickly, before Anthea could give vent to her disappointment. 'But I'm not personally acquainted with the St Clares. I wonder if you would be so good as to tell me something about them?'

Charlotte puckered up her brow consideringly.

'Let me see – well, first of all, *she* is prodigiously lovely, and quite the toast of the Town!'

'Naturally, ma'am, you will be a reliable judge on such a matter,' Justin remarked smiling at her with an intense look that obliged her to lower her eyes, and brought a faint tinge of colour to her cheek.

'Yes, she's very well to pass for a female in her thirties,' put in Anthea, viewing this by-play with sardonic amusement. 'Her hair is brown, to be sure, but it's relieved by reddish tints, and I must own that her figure is prodigiously elegant.'

'My personal preference is for fair colouring,' said Justin, with a meaning look at Charlotte that quite set back her recovery from the effect of his previous compliment. 'However, judging by your description, the lady has certain charms. What of her husband? Is he a handsome, well set up fellow with a dashing address, to match his wife?'

Charlotte laughed. 'Oh, no! At least,' she added fair-mindedly, 'he is most agreeable and quite the gentleman. But he's not one to shine in company, being somewhat withdrawn – some would say too high in the instep. Of course, they *are* a family of ancient lineage, and I collect that his father, the Earl of Pryme, is very conscious of their heritage, and reared his son most strictly never to allow the smallest blot to fall upon the family escutcheon. That would scarce make for ease in social intercourse, would it?'

'No,' agreed Justin. 'And he must have had the deuce of a time of it at Eton or Harrow, or whichever of our schools he graced with his presence. One begins to feel quite sorry for the poor fellow. I rather think I've heard my father speak of Pryme as a starched up kind of character, now I come to think of it.'

At this juncture, the footman announced the arrival of two more visitors, Mr and Miss Blake, and wished to know if Miss Jermyn would see them.

Charlotte gave a ready assent, and Justin politely rose to leave.

'No, pray do stay,' urged Charlotte, waving him back into his chair. 'Anthea knows the Blakes well, for we were both at school with Mary Blake, and I dare say you will be acquainted with her brother Rupert, will you not, sir?'

'Yes, indeed, though he's six years my junior, so we were never in the same set. But are you quite sure you'd like us to stay, Miss Jermyn? We've no wish to intrude.'

For answer she smiled at him so winningly that he at once sat down again, for the moment unable to offer further resistance. Anthea, who had never made the slightest show of departing, grinned wickedly at him so that he longed to box her ears.

Miss Blake was a plain girl, with straight brown hair pinned tightly back into a knot under a straw bonnet trimmed with yellow ribbons which only served to accentuate a somewhat sallow complexion. Her brother was of a similar colouring, but it became him better. His skin was lightly tanned by a sportsman's exposure to wind and weather, his hair was swept back in the fashionable Brutus style and he wore short sideburns. His fawn pantaloons and cinnamon coat were well tailored without being dandified.

Justin was quite accustomed to watching young men falling over themselves to gain Anthea's notice; but on this occasion it was plain that Rupert Blake had eyes for no one but Charlotte. He greeted Anthea as any man might the school friend of his sister, shook hands cordially with Justin and said it was a long time since last they met; and thereafter devoted himself to an attempt to engage most of Miss Jermyn's conversation. She, however, was by far too well mannered to permit this.

Justin began by feeling piqued, but ended by sharing a

covert amusement with Anthea. After a short while, they rose to take their leave. Under Blake's watchful eye, Justin took the hand Charlotte offered and tantalisingly carried it to his lips in old fashioned courtesy. She blushed prettily, an enchanting sight that nevertheless did not entirely prevent Justin from catching the look of naked hostility in Blake's eyes.

'Did you remark the way he looked at you?' Anthea demanded with a chuckle, as they left the house. 'I truly believe he could have murdered you – oh!' She clapped her hand to her mouth in mock dismay.

'Yes, indeed. Tell me, How long has he been hanging out after Miss Jermyn?'

'Oh, I think for several months before the season started. She and Mary have been seeing each other frequently since school, you know, so whenever Rupert Blake chanced to be at home, he would naturally encounter Charlotte. But now that she's come out, of course, they see each other at almost all the balls and parties – not that poor Charlotte will be able to attend any more this season,' she added, compassionately. 'How monstrously boring for her! And all for an uncle who didn't care a rush for her happiness, but tried his utmost to force her to wed that odious Escott!'

'I wonder why?' mused Justin. 'There's the title, and Escott's a warm man, but I'll wager Miss Jermyn could easily enough do better for herself by her uncle's reckoning, once she'd been out for a few months and encountered a wider circle.'

Anthea gave him a sly glance. 'I'm not sure that the youngest brother of a Viscount, even one with a *very easy* competence, would have been considered more eligible,' she quipped.

'No, hussy? You may be right, in which case it's as well that I'm not in the matrimonial stakes.'

'Are you not? Ah, but can you be sure of that?'

He grinned at her. 'Well, there's no saying that one's defences might not – I say only *might*, mark you – be breached in time. However, since your fair friend can't with propriety be considering matrimony herself until the mourning period is past, the danger can be averted. Seriously, though, Anthea, has this fellow made her a declaration, do you know? Or approached her guardian?'

'Oh!' As usual, her quick mind had followed his train of thought. 'Justin, you don't suppose – ? Charlotte did tell me – in the strictest confidence, only I can see that there are times when one must break confidences, and murder is one – that Rupert Blake had applied to Sir Aubrey, who'd refused him permission to approach Charlotte, saying that she was to wed Escott! Which made her furious, only less so than Mr Blake, it seems, who has a monstrous quick temper, and almost came to blows with Sir Aubrey! But surely he wouldn't – Justin, you can't *truly* think that – '

She stopped suddenly in the street, staring at him, appalled.

'Who can say? One must consider every possibility. The largest gap in our information at present is concerned with Jermyn's burial – where the deuce was the man killed? However, Watts and I will be attending to that. As for you, niece – ' he looked at her warningly – 'have a care how you go about tracing the writer of that note. But *if* you can turn up trumps without involving yourself in a scrape, I'll be devilish grateful, I assure you.'

CHAPTER VIII

Stella, Viscountess St Clare, sat alone in the morning room of the family town house, staring dejectedly down into the gardens of Grosvenor Square. An unfinished piece of embroidery lay neglected in her lap, but it was evident that she had no further interest in this, if, indeed, she had taken it up with any real enthusiasm in the first place. She had to be doing something after all; but there was nothing now she wished to do.

Her thoughts went round and round in her head like trapped birds in a cage. If only she had never met him – well, never come to know him intimately. One met everybody in fashionable circles, of course, but an acquaintance need never pass beyond the bowing and greeting stage. That fatal visit to Sussex to stay with the Glynders, people she did not care for above half! But it had been difficult to refuse yet another invitation. They had turned out to be every bit as boring as she had feared they might, too. Very soon that did not signify; nothing signified but the torrent of feeling in which she became engulfed.

What *was* it about him that gave him that fatal power of attraction? He was a good looking man, certainly, but not more so than many others of her acquaintance; and as a woman who was an acknowledged beauty, many such had courted her before. She summoned up an image of him to her mind; his air, address, the way he put his head a little to one side as he gave her a tender, intimate smile –

She broke off in her thoughts, crushing the embroidery between her hands in an agony of mental suffering echoed by the physical as the needle pierced her hand. She was almost glad of the small hurt which recalled her momentarily to the present. He was dead, gone for ever. It was all over.

She knew that he had not been worthy of any sincere regard. He was a libertine, a rake, a womaniser – call him what you will, she thought, nothing would be too harsh. It made no difference. The feeling she had had for him was not of that order; not the true love of poesy nor yet the mature affection which binds a good marriage together. It was an obsession that burnt deep into the emotions, leaving them permanently scarred. Neither was it physical desire alone, although that was a part of it. It required of her a slavish subjection in every thought, word and deed. It was as if no one in the universe existed but this one man; he alone dominated her whole being.

It was like an illness for which there is no cure, she thought. Better that she, too, had died with him. In a sense, she had.

There was a tap on the door, and a footman entered the room. He announced her father-in-law, the Earl of Pryme. She looked up, startled, then rose to her feet to greet him, her embroidery falling to the floor.

He stooped to retrieve it, placing it carelessly on a side table. He was a tall, thin man with a severe expression which did not relent at all as he gave her a formal greeting.

'Be seated, Ma'am,' he said coldly, as she stood before him uncertainly.

She moved towards the chair she had just vacated, but he waved her to one of a pair standing close together.

'Not there – here. I wish to talk to you.'

She caught her breath in dismay. Everyone, including

her husband, had learnt to dread the Earl in such a mood as this. She sat down obediently, and he seated himself beside her.

'What is this nonsense?' he demanded, sharply. 'I observe you've been cancelling your engagements and remaining shut up within doors for the past few days. What ails you?'

'I – I have not been well – '

'Are you breeding again?' he asked, in a brutal tone.

She blushed fiery red, shaking her head.

'This mealy-mouthed generation!' he said, contemptuously. 'I'll have you know, daughter, that I speak plain – aye, and mean to tell you to your head that I am not only aware of your recent shameful liaison, but have kept myself fully informed in that regard from the very first.'

Her lips opened as if she would speak, but no words came.

'Aye, you thought you were secure, I don't doubt. I'll say this, you managed the affair more discreetly than some of his mistresses. That much is to your credit, at all events. Never think though, that you can hoodwink *me*, madam! *I* watch over the honour of my house, even though that fool of a son of mine is as blind as a bat.'

'How – how – did you discover it?' she whispered.

He laughed unpleasantly. 'I'll wager you'd give a deal to know that, madam! Suffice it to say that Pryme can yet command faithful service. But let that pass for the present. I've come here to command you to cease behaving like a lovesick loon. Show yourself about the Town in your usual style at balls, routs and other such gatherings. Appear to be your normally animated self. Go shopping, yes, even to that demmed modiste in Bond Street where you parted with your virtue.'

She flung up a hand as though he had hit her.

'Oh, no, *no*!'

'Yes, yes,' he insisted, thrusting his face close to hers. '*Most of all* you must continue to visit there. You should not need telling that gossip can run like wildfire through the Town. Any singularity of behaviour on your part, and there will be those who are ready to put two and two together and make a sum total of a score. Jermyn was careful, but there may well be others beside my agent to observe him sneak into that side entrance to the modiste's – what's the demmed woman's name? No matter. It won't be her genuine one – and, moreover, to notice that your visits to the shop coincided with his. If your present conduct should lend any colour to such idle observations, you will be a *cause celebre* overnight. And that *I will not permit*, is it understood? The name of Pryme must and shall remain unsmirched, whatever I have found necessary to do in the past to achieve this, and whatever it may yet be necessary to do.'

She stared at him, her countenance horror stricken.

'Whatever you have found necessary – ?' she whispered.

'No matter for that,' he answered harshly. 'Listen well, madam, while I tell you precisely how you must conduct yourself.'

Anthea was feeling frustrated over her failure to verify the authorship of the note which Justin had entrusted to her. No matter that it had been in her possession only a few days and already she was reasonably certain that it had been written by Stella St Clare. Suspicion was not proof, and she had been deeply disappointed that Charlotte could not produce a sample of the lady's handwriting.

Her fertile mind produced a number of daring schemes to achieve her purpose; but mature consideration reluctantly rejected these as impracticable. She had always complained that females were by far too hedged about with convention. There seemed no sense in it. One might not venture into the street without the escort of a male or female companion, or else one's maid. One dared not walk down St James's Street, where the gentlemen's clubs were situated, without at once being condemned as 'fast'. One could not allow the same partner to lead one out for a second time at Almack's without eyebrows being raised, or join in the waltz there without the permission of the patronesses. The list was endless, and odiously boring!

Considerations of a similar nature presented monstrous difficulties to a young lady who wished to obtain access to a house where her family had never been in the habit of paying social calls. Moreover, no help could be expected from Charlotte, as she was – officially, at any rate – in mourning at present, and the conventions debarred her from all forms of giddy dissipation.

Anthea chuckled as the phrase came to mind in connection with stuffy social calls. It all went to show how stupid the conventions were.

After all this frantic cudgelling of her wits, at last an idea came to her, so simple that she wondered she had not thought of it before. She had forgotten that the St Clares lived in Grosvenor Square, as also did Lady Quainton, who was Justin's godmother and a very dear friend of Anthea's dead grandmother. It was unlikely that Cassandra Quainton would not be on calling terms with so near a neighbour as Stella St Clare. Moreover, Lady Quainton was already in Justin's confidence about the Jermyn affair.

She decided to go there at once, and was fortunate enough to find Cassandra Quainton at home.

'What a terrifying girl you are, to be sure,' said the latter affectionately, when Anthea had explained her purpose. 'Well, I dare say it won't come amiss to *call* upon Lady St Clare, as I understand she's been cancelling her engagements lately owing to an indisposition, so it would be only neighbourly to enquire how she does. But as to *seeing* her, that doesn't seem very likely, since she's unwell.'

'Has she indeed been cancelling her engagements?' Anthea asked, with interest. 'Well, that adds substance to our suspicions, don't you see, for I know she's aware of Jermyn's murder, as Lady Jermyn received a card of condolence from her yesterday. Oh, that was no use at all,' she added, in response to a questioning look from her hostess. 'It was one of those formal cards, and Justin thought had been filled in by a secretary. It was not in a female hand at all.'

'One cannot but compassionate her somewhat, if indeed she is guilty,' said Lady Quainton. 'Jermyn was an accomplished and unscrupulous rake, you know – and I fear she must find her husband a dead bore. Not that anything can excuse adultery,' she finished, feeling she might have gone too far.

Anthea ignored the moral precept. 'Yes, not only was Sir Aubrey all you say, but he was an odious man besides, as his niece Charlotte could tell you. Trying to force her into a marriage with Lord Escott! Really, one cannot help but feel that he's better dead, and that whoever did it cannot be altogether blamed.'

'My dear child,' reproved Cassandra Quainton, drily, 'some of your notions show a sad lack of proper feeling, I fear. One cannot countenance murder. After all, if people were to take it into their heads to make away with everyone who is odious, or behaves ill, Town would be remarkably thin of company.'

'Well, Justin means to find out the murderer, at all events, because Charlotte has begged him to solve the mystery. He's vastly taken with Charlotte.'

Lady Quainton pricked up her ears. 'Is he so?'

Anthea laughed. 'Don't refine too much upon it, though. I've seen it happen before. I think Justin, like myself, values his freedom.'

'Freedom may seem attractive when one is very young, and has an endless vista of balls and parties stretching ahead. Later, it could be a synonym for loneliness. But I must not prose.'

She walked over to the window and looked out.

'There's Pryme's carriage just leaving the St Clares. I saw him arrive about half an hour since. Perhaps, my dear, we might venture to call now, though I warn you that we're unlikely to be received. I shall of course leave my card with a suitable message, but that won't avail you anything.'

Anthea at once darted to the mirror to don her bonnet, which she had carelessly dropped on the sofa beside her when she arrived. Lady Quainton could not help laughing at her young friend's eagerness as they left the house together.

To the surprise of both, they were almost instantly admitted to the parlour where Stella St Clare was sitting. She rose to greet them readily enough; but Anthea noticed that her smile was forced, her cheeks pale, and her air one of fatigue.

'Pray forgive us if we are disturbing you, Lady St Clare,' began Cassandra Quainton, in her most disarming way. 'Hearing you were indisposed, I meant but to enquire after your health. However, your butler insisted that he had orders not to deny visitors today, so I thought I would just look in and see how you did.'

'How very kind of you!' exclaimed Stella St Clare, in a somewhat forced, gushing manner. 'Yes, I find myself so much better today that I thought it would be of benefit to receive calls again. Pray to be seated, ladies. Can I procure anything for your refreshment? I'll ring the bell directly.'

She started to rise hastily, but Lady Quainton put out a hand to detain her.

'No, thank you, we require nothing, and have no desire to set you in a bustle. No doubt you should be resting as you have been unwell, so we shall stay only a few minutes.'

'Oh, but I'm quite, quite recovered now! You know how it is with these sudden onsets of malaise – one feels like death one day, and perfectly restored the next! Indeed, I find myself so much better that I was just about to send a message to Lady Hertford to say that I shall be able to attend her rout this evening, after all. Do you go to it, either of you?'

Lady Quainton agreed that she would be there, but Anthea shook her head. Isabella, Lady Hertford, was a handsome woman in her fifties to whom the Princess Regent was very attached; but she was too stately and formal for her entertainments to be in the style of the younger generation.

'But pray don't let us interrupt you if you wish to write a note,' added Anthea, earnestly. 'We'll be quite content to sit quietly by while you do so.'

Stella St Clare looked surprised; as well she might, thought Cassandra Quainton in amusement.

'But of course I would not behave in so shabby a fashion!' she protested. 'I shall have time enough later.'

'As to that,' said Anthea, frankly, 'I always think letters should be written when the spirit moves one, otherwise they tend to be overlooked. And since Lady Hertford's rout is this very evening, you would not wish for any delay, would you?'

Cassandra Quainton directed a warning look at her impulsive young companion. This was going too far.

Under her watchful eye, Anthea subsided sufficiently to sustain a reluctant part in the polite social chit chat which followed before they took their leave.

'Oh, *why* would you not let me urge her to write that note?' she complained, bitterly, as they walked the few steps to Lady Quainton's house. 'It would have settled the business splendidly!'

'My dear, I'm sure your male relatives would have told you that you were doing it much too brown. Even in her distracted state, she must have realised you had some purpose, had you said any more.'

'*You* thought she was distracted, too?'

'Yes, indeed. She was obviously a good deal upset underneath that forced amiability towards us. I wonder – if what you and Justin suspect should be indeed the truth, and her indisposition the result of grief over Jermyn's death – then Pryme's visit might have been to warn her not to parade it before the world. He is certainly not the man to trouble himself over the matter of his daughter-in-law's health in the normal way. He's a cold fish, and cares only for the family name.'

'That seems very likely to me,' agreed Anthea. 'And I tell you what, ma'am, I've just had the most famous notion!'

Lady Quainton sighed, being somewhat acquainted with Anthea's famous notions.

'I shall watch from your window for the footman going out with a letter from her house to deliver at Lady Hertford's!' declared Anthea. 'And then I shall – ' she paused uncertainly – 'well, I'll find some way to get a sight of it,' she finished, somewhat lamely.

'But how, my dear? You cannot ask him for it, you know, nor could you very well snatch it from his hand,' objected her companion, reasonably.

'Oh, if only I were a man!' stormed Anthea.

'You would make a vastly poor specimen with that slim figure and piquant face. Believe me, you do much better as a female.'

'Oh, please don't tease me, ma'am – I need to think!'

They had entered the house; but instead of going

towards the staircase to reach the drawing room, Anthea pushed open the door of the front parlour on the ground floor.

'I shall watch from here, if I may, ma'am,' she said, indicating a chair close to the window. 'And I'll require Martha, my maid, to be ready to accompany me out of doors as soon as I give the word. You won't object, ma'am, if I tell her to wait on a chair in the hall?'

Lady Quainton good humouredly acceded to these requests, knowing full well that Anthea must have her way. Martha was summoned from the kitchen, where she had been tea drinking with one or two of the senior staff, and instructed accordingly. Then Anthea sat herself down to watch with keen, bright eyes for any sign of activity from the St Clare's residence.

She had been sitting there little more than a quarter of an hour when she jumped up excitedly.

'A footman's just come out of the house!' she exclaimed. 'And – yes! He's placing a piece of paper carefully in his pocket! I must go, ma'am – pray forgive me – I'll come back and take a proper leave of you later!'

'But, Anthea, my child, do not rush out after the servant in that harum-scarum manner! Wait – '

It was too late. Anthea, bearing her flustered maid before her, had dashed through the hall and down the steps into the Square.

The footman, a youth of about eighteen clad in the cinnamon and fawn livery of the St Clare household, evidently intended to make the most of this unexpected respite from indoor duties on such a warm, pleasant day.

He stepped out briskly enough in traversing the Square, no doubt mindful that the eyes of his superiors might be upon him; but once he had turned into Duke Street, he dawdled along, taking a keen interest in every passing sight and eyeing each girl bound on errands who had any remote claim to good looks.

Anthea and her maid Martha found it quite easy to keep pace with him; and, as the pavement was thronged with people, he paid not the slightest heed to the two females close at his heels.

Meanwhile, Anthea's mind was working furiously. How could she possibly obtain possession of that note, if only for a few moments? The only way she could see would be to pick his pocket, and she doubted her skill at this. If only it were possible to distract him in some way; if only Martha had been a saucy young creature of his own age, instead of someone old enough to be his mother. But then, she reflected inconsequentially, Mama would never have appointed one such to act as her maid. She must simply keep on following the youth, and hope for something advantageous to occur.

Her fervent wishes were answered when they reached the junction with Oxford Street. A ragged man was standing against a wall on the corner playing a fiddle. Quite a little crowd had gathered about him, caught up in the music – a porter who had set down the trunk he was carrying for a brief rest, a broadsheet seller, a baker with his basket on his back, a grimy chimney sweep, a pretty girl from one of the milliner's with a bandbox on her arm, and several boys jigging about in time to the tune. The footman joined them, pushing his way through to a place beside the milliner's apprentice. She turned towards him with a provocative smile, and his interest quickened.

Seeing his preoccupation, Anthea also pushed her way into the crowd until she was close behind him. Swiftly, but gently, she slid the note out of his pocket.

He gave no sign, too taken up with the girl at his side, who was giving saucy answers to his attempts to improve their acquaintance. Anthea sidled out of the crowd, the note firmly grasped in her hand, and retreated into a nearby archway beside a shop. Martha followed, not understanding what was going forward, but too accustomed to Miss Anthea's vagaries to raise any protest.

Anthea glanced quickly at the note, confirmed that it was directed to the Marchioness of Hertford, then handed it to Martha.

'Hold this for a moment, please,' she said, sliding her reticule from her left wrist.

Martha obeyed, goggle-eyed, while Anthea took out Stella St Clare's note to Jermyn, placing it side by side with the letter purloined from the footman. The handwriting was identical.

Anthea drew a deep breath, replacing the original note in her reticule.

It had taken only a few moments. When she once more insinuated herself into the crowd, the footman had improved his acquaintance with the milliner's assistant to a degree when he noticed nothing as Anthea restored the note to his pocket.

Not until they were on their way back to Grosvenor Square did the long-suffering Martha at last give voice to a mild protest.

'Lud, Miss Anthea, what starts you do get up to! Milady would have a fit if she knew the half!'

'I dare say,' replied her mistress coolly. 'But since I don't intend to inform her and I *think* I can rely upon you not to peach on me, her health should mercifully remain unimpaired.'

'*Think*, indeed?' repeated Martha, hurt. 'You know very well, miss, I'd rather cut off my right hand than betray you, come what may!'

'Dear Martha, I hope it would never come to that,' replied Anthea with a warm smile, as she pressed the maid's arm. 'There's no one like you, I declare! And I may tell you – in *strictest* confidence, mind – that this time it isn't just one of my wild starts, but a matter that concerns the Law. I mean,' she added, hastily, realising that in the circumstances this was an equivocal statement, 'I mean that we've been *assisting* the Law, you and I, unlikely though it may seem.'

CHAPTER IX

Towards midnight, two disreputable figures, indistinguishable in the murky gloom from the rest of those frequenting that sleazy quarter, might have been seen making their way towards the Artichoke public house in Southwark.

A strong stomach was needed to traverse this warren of dark lanes and narrow alleyways with foul smelling gutters running along them, and indescribably filthy refuse strewn everywhere. The tenements and hovels which crowded on all sides were blackened with age – old grime; doors hung drunkenly from rusty, broken hinges, and windows had straw or rags stuffed into the gaps left by shattered panes of glass.

Here and there a flight of broken stone steps led down to the horrors of a dingy cellar where two or three families eked out a squalid existence. Small groups were often gathered at the top of these steps, seemingly having emerged from below to take a breather; though it was scarcely possible that the tainted air outside could be any improvement on the stale atmosphere of what was thought of as home by these poor wretches. The groups consisted of slatternly women and miserable children in filthy rags which only partly covered their emaciated bodies. It seemed that the men had business elsewhere.

On reaching the first of these dejected groups, one of the

two men passing by swore graphically under his breath, his hand reaching instinctively for his pocket to afford them some means of relief. Before the compassionate action could betray him, his companion seized his wrist in a firm grip.

'For God's sake, no! D'ye mean to bring the whole stinkin' populace about our ears?'

Justin nodded. Watts was in the right of it, of course. They had been warned at the Union Street police office in Southwark – though such a warning was scarcely necessary to Watts – that this was a dangerous quarter for anyone who showed the slightest sign of being above the prevailing company of cut throats, thieves, slatterns and the sweepings of the local streets. They had taken great pains with their disguise, too; even going to the length of grubbing around in Justin's coal cellar to give the final touches to the set of miserable rags which Watts had managed to provide for the purpose.

'If only ye'll remember not to open y'r mouth, sir,' Watts had pleaded, when they were ready to start.

'Devil take it. I can talk slum cant with the best!'

'Mebbe ye knows the words, sir, but 'tis the tone, d'ye see? Officer, not other ranks, if ye takes my meaning.'

They finally reached their objective, almost staggering before the blast of foetid air which greeted them from the open door of the tavern. They rallied quickly, pushing their way through the rough looking customers crowding the taproom, most of them already the worse for drink. One or two had a slatternly female hanging from his arm, but for the most part, the Artichoke was a male haunt.

After some jostling and free use of foul language from those surrounding them, they managed to procure a pot of ale apiece, as being less lethal than the gin which was in more popular demand.

'Reckon this'll rot our guts, too,' whispered Watts, as

they shouldered their way out of the press round the tap into a less dense, though still crowded part of the small room. 'Still, won't do to go empty fisted in a boozing ken.'

Justin did his best not to survey the contents of his mug with strong distaste, managing this tolerably well by turning a heavy scowl upon his inoffensive companion instead.

They found a section of the wall against which to lean their shoulders, and unobtrusively subjected the customers about them to a close scrutiny. They had been given a good description of the man whom they were seeking, one Ben Crouch, thought to be the leader of the Borough Boys gang; but owing to the press of customers filling the taproom and overflowing into an adjacent cubby hole which was without a door, it was some time before they caught sight of him.

Justin saw him first, and gave Watts a nudge. His glance directed the Runner to a typically seedy character with a badly pock marked face and a leering expression. The man was sitting with a group of others on rickety stools in the crowded cubby hole, deep in tipsy conversation punctuated by an occasional loud guffaw. There seemed small chance of isolating him from his fellows.

Customers were constantly pushing their way to and from the smaller room, where Justin could just manage to espy a door which would most likely lead out into the back yard.

An idea came to him. He communicated it to the Runner's ear under cover of the din surrounding them.

Watts nodded. Together they elbowed their way amongst the others into the adjacent room to a spot close beside their quarry. Once there, Watts deftly nudged the elbow of the man sitting next to this individual at the table, causing him to spill his drink over the table and on to his nether garments.

Pock face jumped up in fury and landed his neighbour a facer.

In such congested quarters and among men inflamed by alcohol, this was only the beginning of a very promising scrap. Before long, everyone was hitting out at those around him indiscriminatingly.

Justin and Watts managed to keep close behind their man, almost using him as a shield until an appropriate moment came for Justin to fell him with a punch which might have earned even the great Gentleman Jackson's approbation. Between them, he and Watts half dragged the unconscious man away from the thick of the fray towards the exit. No one heeded them, as all were too busy with their own concerns.

Here, however, they suffered a set-back for a few moments, falling foul of a group of rogues already engaged in a ferocious struggle. They were obliged to drop their burden and defend themselves in earnest. Watts produced his truncheon and laid about him with a will, so soon those who were still able to stand turned their aggression elsewhere.

'Sharp's the word!' uttered Watts, seizing the recumbent form they had abandoned.

Justin kicked open the door. Together, they bundled their burden through it, slamming it shut behind them. A couple of kegs stood close by in the yard. Unceremoniously dumping the inert body on the ground, they pushed these in front of the door.

Somewhat breathless, they turned to look around the yard, illuminated feebly by a lamp hanging from a bracket over the door. A delapidated shed stood against the wall a few yards away. They dragged their captive inside. He began to stir as they propped him up against the wall.

'That's the dandy!' said Watts, approvingly. 'Open

them pretty ogles o'yourn!'

He gave the man a couple of smart slaps across his face. The victim shook his head, growled, then started to his feet aggressively.

'Oh, no you don't,' said Justin, softly, pinning his arms. 'Don't be alarmed – we only want you to answer a few questions.'

A stream of foul invective greeted this. Watts drew out his truncheon, flourishing it menacingly.

'The law, me cully. And if ye don't choose to open that mummer o' yourn to good purpose, I'll not be answerable for the consequences. See?'

It took a little time for the rogue to see. Eventually, he began to talk; but Justin, for all his boasted knowledge of thieves' cant, found he was unable to understand more than a few words without a glossary.

'We begin to make progress, Joe,' remarked Justin.

It was the following morning, and they both presented their normal appearance to the world. Inevitably they had suffered battle scars, but fortunately these were concealed by clothing, with no betraying facial injuries.

They considered that the results fully compensated for any temporary physical discomfort. The man Crouch had finally yielded to persuasion and divulged the site of the burial ground from which Jermyn's body had been snatched, as well as the name of the gravedigger there.

Watts had just returned from an interview with this individual.

'Pure as any angel, sir, by his reckoning. He only did a favour for a poor cully who told a sad tale of how his sister'd done away with herself, and the family wished to bury her nice and quiet, like. So he dug a hole for the interment, then let 'em in after dark to do the business. Three of 'em, he said. Swore at first he didn't know any of 'em – man gave his name as Smith – *Smith*, I ask ye, sir! But after I pressed him a trifle, he admitted that he'd seen Smith somewhere before. *Where* d'ye think, guv'nor?'

Justin smiled. 'I'll not be caught like that, Joe. I'm sure you're all agog to inform me.'

'Well, it was at a saddler's in the Borough High Street, not far from the burial ground.'

'Carter, eh? Too much of a coincidence for it to be another saddler's, but we'll check that, damned if we won't. Tell me, when did this burial take place?'

'On the Monday that deceased disappeared – ten days since, that's to say.'

'So he was killed that same day. It seemed likely from the first. And we know from Astley Cooper that the resurrectionists snatched the body on the following Friday. Had the gravedigger any convincing explanation to offer as to how they came to be aware of a recent burial, or to gain access to the burial ground in his charge?'

'What d'ye think, sir? He claims they possess a set of bettys – picklocks, that is – will get 'em in anywhere. Mebbe so, but I reckon they didn't need to use tools. I'll wager they greased him well enough in the fist to assist their nefarious trade.'

'Undoubtedly. And now I think we should proceed to Southwark. But we'll take a hackney for that quarter.'

Presently they alighted from this humble and not particularly clean vehicle in the Borough High Street, paid off the jarvey, and looked about them. They soon identified the saddler's premises from the description given to Watts. It was a small shop beside a narrow, dark entry. As they approached it, Justin gave a sharp exclamation.

'Damme! See what the neighbouring place is?'

Watts looked, and raised his eyebrows when he discovered that the premises on the opposite side of the entry belonged to an undertaker.

'I'll take that one,' said Justin, striding purposefully towards it.

He pushed open the door and entered a small, rather dim room. Before he had time to look about him, a man appeared wearing a carpenter's apron under a black coat which had evidently been hastily donned, for the lining of one sleeve was hanging down over his hand. He pushed it back and, having scrutinised his customer shrewdly, bowed obsequiously.

'Good day to you, y'r honour. Is there some way in which I may serve you?'

'There may well be,' replied Justin. 'I see it is your business to supply coffins and arrange for interments.'

'That is so, sir. Let me hasten to express my sympathy in the sad loss which I suppose you to have sustained, and to recommend to your honour the wrought-iron coffin which is my own particular patent, and which is the only surety against the wicked despoilers of graveyards who perpetrate unspeakable crimes against the earthly remains of dear ones who are mourned by sorrowing relatives. My iron coffin is a mere ten guineas, y'r honour, and what is such a trifling sum to a gentleman like you, compared to the horrors of bodysnatching?'

'What indeed?' echoed Justin, raising a hand to check this unlooked for eloquence. 'But I'm not here to engage your offices in a professional capacity, my good man, but to make a few inquiries of you concerning a wooden coffin which you supplied to another recently.'

The man raised his head sharply and gave Justin a wary look.

'A complaint, is it? Let me assure you that all my boxes are made from the stoutest – '

'No, no such thing,' said Justin hurriedly, to avoid further sales talk. 'I dare say your work is all that you claim for it. That doesn't concern me. What I wish to know is, did you supply a coffin ten days ago – a Monday – at the request of a man named Carter, who works at the saddler's next door?'

The undertaker bridled. 'Indeed I did, sir, though it's by no means pleasing to me to be called on for funerary furniture when I'm not in charge of the interment. A shabby business it would be, too, I'll be bound, with him choosing the cheapest – not but what,' he added, reluctant to let slip a chance of promoting his goods, 'that our cheapest bain't a sight better than most.'

'A deal better, in fact?' said Justin with a grin. 'But never mind my poor puns. I'm vastly obliged to you for the information. Would you mind telling me whether Carter himself collected the coffin, or instructed you to deliver it somewhere?'

'He paid to have it delivered to the burial ground near St Thomas's,' replied the undertaker. 'But what's your interest in all this, y'r honour?' he asked, his glance sharpening. 'I don't rightly see how it concerns you.'

'Possibly not, but perhaps this – ' Justin placed a couple of sovereigns on the counter – 'may recompense you for your wasted time.'

The man swept up the money quickly, a gleam in his eye.

'One more question only,' continued Justin. 'Can you recollect at what time of day Carter came here to bespeak the coffin?'

The man considered for a moment. 'Not precisely, but it must have been something after five, I reckon, for I'd not long had my dinner, that I do remember. Say about six.'

Justin nodded. In his circles, it was customary to partake of dinner later in the evening, but he was familiar with the habits of ordinary folk.

'I grumbled at being called on to supply goods at such short notice,' went on the undertaker, 'and I had to charge according, which is only right, also for delivery after dark, into the bargain. Come to think of it,' he added, 'I don't rightly know how he found the blunt, in his line of work. But it mightn't have been for him, but for someone else – he didn't say, nor I didn't ask.'

'Understandable. Well, I thank you for your assistance. Good day.'

He left the shop just as Watts emerged from next door.

'Our man's slung his hook, seemingly,' the Runner greeted him. 'Not been in to work this week at all, though his employer says that's no great loss. I asked if he was there all day on the Monday of deceased's disappearance, and he was, right enough, until seven o'clock in the evening. I reckon I scared him off when I questioned Madam's workers on Sunday, and he was unlucky enough to be with his moll, the girl Bates at the time. We'll find him easy enough through her, though, if we want him.'

'And assuredly we shall.'

Justin related his conversation with the undertaker. Watts whistled.

'Corroborative evidence, eh? D'ye reckon Carter did the murder? Yes, and now I recollect where I've seen that cully before! He was one of three men brought in to Bow Street for suspected housebreaking some months back. No conviction, on account of the householder couldn't swear to 'em, and they didn't get away with any swag, so he refused to prosecute. Y'know how it is, sir – prosecutions cost money and waste a mort o'time, so folks won't trouble themselves unless they stand to regain valuables. That lot weren't up to milling a ken,' he added, disparagingly. 'More like rampsmen or prigs.'

'Footpads or pickpockets, what?' translated Justin. 'So Carter's not above turning his hand to crime. I wonder if those same confederates assisted him in the burial of Jermyn's body? I don't quite see a motive for murder, though – would they use a pistol for robbery?'

Watts shook his head. 'Rampsmen don't use barkers. A cosh is their weapon.'

'There's no proof that Jermyn wasn't robbed, of course, since his body was unclothed. But it strains probability to suppose that Carter or one of his confederates would shoot and rob their victim, then afterwards spend some of the proceeds on a burial. Why not leave the body *in situ*, as it were, and decamp hastily?'

Watts grinned. 'Put like that, sir – '

'Yes, absurd. But you know, Watts, all the evidence suggest to me that Jermyn never left the modiste's premises, but was murdered somewhere there. That would rule out Carter, as you're informed he was at work at the saddler's all day on the Monday in question.'

'True. You think deceased was killed at Madam's, too, do you, sir? So do I. Consider the evidence. He made a firm arrangement with the jarvey for four o'clock, yet never appeared. I got the crossing sweeper to vouch for the jarvey's story, and the lad also said that he'd not seen anyone emerge from Madam's private street entrance for some time before the jarvey arrived. Besides, why should deceased leave his lady love before he'd intended?'

Justin frowned. 'Unless an emergency arose. But even so, there are only two other exits he could have used. One is the salon, which he certainly would not have chosen at any cost. The other is the basement and yard exit through the mews, and the workpeople there denied seeing him when you interrogated them. Not that it would be impossible to escape observation, though. It would be helpful to know when Jermyn's lady visitor departed, but at present we've not even ascertained her identity. Find Carter, Joe, and we'll be able to progress a little further, at any rate.'

CHAPTER X

Lady Jermyn sat opposite her niece at the breakfast table, her brows drawn into a frown as she perused a letter that had arrived that morning.

Although she was dressed in black as convention decreed, she looked a great deal better, more composed and less pale than when she had first heard the news of her husband's death. Charlotte had been pleased to see the change in her over the past few days, and was considering making a suggestion that they should both drive out in the Park after breakfast.

'Is there something tiresome in your letter, Aunt Amelia?' she asked, sympathetically.

'It is from Mr Leasowe, your uncle's man of business, my dear. It says – but perhaps you had best read it for yourself.'

She passed the letter across the table. Charlotte read it attentively, then handed it back.

'I realized that this Mr George Jermyn would inherit the baronetcy, of course,' she said, slowly. 'But I knew nothing of an entail – indeed, how should I, for my uncle would never have discussed such matters with me.'

'I may say that he had never mentioned them even to me,' replied Lady Jermyn, not without some indignation in her tone. 'And now it seems that we must lose Wynsfield, together with the income from the land belonging to it! It was a great deal too bad of Aubrey – ' she pulled herself up short, realising the impropriety of such a comment. 'That's to say,' she concluded, more mildly, 'I dare say it wouldn't have occurred to him to discuss matters of a business nature with a female, even his wife. Gentlemen in general never do so, you know.'

Charlotte nodded. 'Yes, but it's an antiquated notion, Aunt Amelia, for many females are extremely practical, else how should they manage their households so well?'

'Oh, that is different, being purely of a domestic nature. Besides, I know of several who have no notion whatsoever of management, but leave all in the hands of the housekeeper. Of course a clever, bookish girl like yourself would not be satisfied without playing an active part in something or other, and I dare say you'll run your establishment to perfection when you are married.'

'Hmm,' remarked Charlotte drily. 'Well, we shall see. But does this mean that we'll be paupers, Aunt?'

'Oh, no!' exclaimed Lady Jermyn, shocked. 'No such thing! At least – you see that Mr Leasowe says he intends to wait upon us tomorrow, if that should be convenient, and explain the situation more fully. He also begs leave to introduce your uncle's relative, Mr – I should say Sir, of course – George Jermyn, to us. It seems that the new baronet desires to make our acquaintance. Very proper, I must say.'

'He is some kind of distant cousin, is he not?'

'He's the only son of your uncle's cousin – and of your father's, too, come to that. Ah, if only your papa had survived, he would have inherited,' Lady Jermyn added, sadly.

Charlotte was not the kind of girl to dwell upon might-have-beens, so she ignored this.

'I suppose if the worst overtakes us, I could go for a governess,' she said brightly. 'But I fear my knowledge of the globes is not all it might be, while my needlework is no more than passable. Only think of that firescreen I embroidered – now deservedly come to rest in one of the attics! If I unpicked that design once, I did so a dozen times, and in the end it was lopsided!'

'But you were only fourteen, dearest, and indeed I thought it very pretty,' insisted her aunt loyally. 'I would have kept it in the small parlour, you know, but your uncle – '

'Dear Aunt Amelia, you're always ready to make allowances for everyone. I don't at all blame Uncle Aubrey for refusing to live with such an eyesore, though.'

'One cannot hurt a child's feelings, especially when so much effort has been put into a piece of work. But of course it's nonsense for you to talk of being obliged to earn a living for yourself! Things are not come to such a pass, I hope, though our income may be somewhat reduced. However, Mr Leasowe will make all clear to us tomorrow. I wonder,' she continued after a pause, 'whether your uncle had any thought of such a contingency as this in mind when he was so insistent upon a match between you and Lord Escott? In worldly terms, it would be a most advantageous marriage, and your future would be secure.'

'Never say *you* intend to plague me on that subject!' exclaimed Charlotte, in disgust.

'Oh, no, my love – I would not for the world have you wed without affection, for nothing is more melancholy. But I was only trying to account for your uncle's determined support of Escott's suit, and that did seem a likely reason for it.'

'Not to me. I shall never believe that he cared a rush for my welfare. No, I think it more probable that either he himself stood to gain in some way from such a marriage, or else – ' She broke off, frowning.

'Or else?' queried Lady Jermyn.

'Or else that Lord Escott had some kind of hold over him, so that he was anxious to fall in with whatever the odious monster suggested!'

She eyed her aunt warily after this outburst, fearing that she might have gone too far, loving and tolerant though Lady Jermyn invariably was towards her.

To her surprise, the older woman nodded.

'It's odd you should say that, because something of the kind has more than once crossed my mind, Lottie, I must confess. Theirs was a curious friendship, more like a –' she paused to consider – 'a business connection. They were not in the same set, for Escott isn't one of the Prince Regent's intimates, and they were a generation apart in age, which meant they rarely shared sporting activities. Yet I know that Aubrey spent a certain amount of time at Escott's house in St James's Square more or less regularly, and Escott used to come here occasionally, when the two of them would be closeted together in the bookroom. Latterly, of course, Escott came here to court you, so his visits were more social than before – dinner parties and the like.'

Charlotte made a grimace, but said nothing.

'I could never think what they found to discuss so earnestly, unless it might have been horseflesh,' continued Lady Jermyn. 'They were both addicted to racing, I do know – indeed, to most forms of gaming. But I don't believe they truly liked each other above half. Yes, and now I come to think of it, I remember once Aubrey laughing and saying that on one occasion he had got the better of Escott, at any rate. I asked what he meant, but he wouldn't tell me any more, save to say that it was long ago in Brighton. Before we were married, my dear – ' she sighed – 'he spent a deal of time at Wynsfield, I collect, as it's so near Brighton, which during the season is just the town for wild young bucks. That part of his life is a closed book to me, though. He was never the man for confidential exchanges, nor raking over the past. Indeed – perhaps I should not say this, even to you – I never felt that we were as close as man and wife should be. Perhaps it was because we had no children. Children draw couples together.'

'Not always, I think.'

Lady Jermyn seized her hand in an agony of remorse.

'Oh, my dearest Lottie, pray forgive me! You have been *my own* dear daughter – never have I thought of you in any other way. I only meant – '

Charlotte patted the hand reassuringly.

'I know what you meant, my love, so don't fear for my sensibilities. *You* thought of me as your own child, but it was quite otherwise with Uncle Aubrey. Do you honestly think that real parenthood would have brought him any closer to you? I wonder.'

'I cannot blame him, for evidently there was something lacking in myself,' said Lady Jermyn, sadly. 'That was why he always needed the reassurance of some other female – oh, yes, I know of his many amours. How could I not, with the Town talking of them for ever?'

'The only think lacking in *you*, dearest, is a true appreciation of your own worth!' exploded her niece. 'As for my uncle – ! Well, *de mortuis*, I suppose,' she added, grudgingly, 'though why death should turn people into plaster saints, I for one cannot imagine! And now I'm going to take you for a drive, as I think it high time you should have some fresh air and company.'

'This is indeed an honour,' said Justin to his two lady visitors that afternoon. 'Pray be seated, Godmama. I think you will find that armchair reasonably comfortable. As for you, niece, I'm sure you'll decide on a perch for yourself, when you have done prancing about the room.'

Anthea removed her attractive straw bonnet trimmed

with ruched cherry ribbons, and ran her fingers impatiently through her dark curls.

'I only prance, as you style it, because I'm impatient to tell you that I've solved the mystery of the note you entrusted to me! Have I not done well? But you shall hear the whole.'

She seated herself on the sofa, tossing the bonnet down beside her.

'Splendid! But as it may be a long recital, shall I first order some refreshment for you? Tea, Godmama? Or would you prefer lemonade or ratafia?'

This offer having been accepted and attended to, Anthea proceeded to plunge into her tale. When she reached the point where she had tried to urge Stella St Clare to write the note to Lady Hertford immediately, Justin chuckled, and shook his head.

'That was pitching it too rum,' he said. 'Small wonder if the lady had smelt a rat.'

'Why, so I told her,' agreed Lady Quainton. 'Fortunately, Stella St Clare was in too troubled a frame of mind to take particular notice, though she did look a trifle shocked at the suggestion.'

'As things turned out, it didn't matter that I couldn't persuade her,' continued Anthea. 'It was like this, you see – '

Her recital of the ensuing chase and her capture of Stella St Clare's letter lost none of its drama in the telling.

'Good Lord, I couldn't do better at Covent Garden!' exclaimed Justin, laughing. 'But seriously, Anthea, you took a devilish risk of being apprehended as a prig and hauled off to Bow Street.'

'Prig?' queried Cassandra Quainton.

'Thieves' cant, Godmama,' apologised Justin. 'I fear I'm catching it from Runner Joseph Watts. We've both been keeping low company lately. Well, Anthea, you've certainly done well – I should have been at point non plus without your assistance.'

She looked pleased at this, and rose to drop him a mocking curtsy.

'But that's not all,' she continued, 'for Aunt Cassandra – ' a courtesy title among the female Rutherfords for their dead grandmother's very dear friend – 'heard some useful gossip from her maid just before we set out for a drive in the Park, later on. Oh, and we met Charlotte and her aunt – '

Lady Quainton held up a hand for silence. 'I consider you to have had enough of the limelight for the present, my dear, and I positively insist on telling that part of the story myself.'

'I am all ears,' promised Justin, grinning.

'Well, not quite, though they do protrude a fraction,' remarked Anthea, judicially. 'However, it's said to be a sign of originality, you know.'

'You reassure me. And now pray allow my Godmama to relate her news, or I shall be obliged to assault you with the ruler lying on my writing desk.'

Anthea wrinkled her nose at him.

'It chances that my abigail Jane and Lady St Clare's Ruth are bosom bows,' began Lady Quainton. 'I would like to think that Jane is a trifle more scrupulous than Ruth, for the latter is given to listening at doors, as you shall soon learn. During the Earl of Pryme's visit to Stella St Clare this morning, the maid's ear seems to have been applied to good purpose. She was able to repeat almost every word of their conversation to my abigail.'

Justin listened attentively while she reported it.

'Hmm. Pryme, what? Not the husband, but the head of the family, reproves the erring wife. From what Miss Jermyn told us, Pryme would go to some lengths to safeguard the family honour. But murder?'

'If the maid heard aright, he made a remark tantamount to a confession,' Anthea reminded him.

'You refer to "Whatever I've found it necessary to do in the past"? True, but that could mean on other occasions. Nevertheless, it may be profitable to trace Pryme's movements on the afternoon we've reason to believe the murder took place. There are others, too.'

'You mean you know when it was? I thought you'd no notion what had occurred between the Monday of Sir Aubrey's disappearance and the finding of his dead body several days later.'

Justin thought rapidly. There was no point in harrowing the two females with the grisly story of the interment and the body snatching. It might have to be disclosed before the investigation was concluded, but meanwhile it was wiser to keep to the secrecy Astley Cooper had enjoined towards the bereaved family. On the other hand, it was as well that these two invaluable informants should be made aware of the present state of the case.

'Runner Watts and I have been working on that gap in our information, and we've now established that the murder took place on the very afternoon when you observed Jermyn at the salon,' he answered her. '*Where* it occurred is not yet clear. At present Watts is looking for a man who has prudently removed himself from his known haunts – a man connected with one of Madame Yvonne's seamstresses, and who certainly knows the answer to that question.'

'Madame Yvonne's seamstresses!' echoed Anthea. 'Upon my word, you're being odiously cryptic, Justin! I would like to hear the whole!'

'I dare say he has good reason for his reticence,' put in Cassandra Quainton. 'But tell me, Justin, do you then suspect that the murder took place somewhere on Madame Yvonne's premises, and that the body was afterwards removed to the place where it was found?'

Justin nodded. 'The time-table of events does suggest that. Runner Watts has established that Jermyn arranged with a hackney coachman to be picked up at four o'clock sharp outside the private entrance to the shop premises. Both this coachman and the crossing sweeper affirm that Jermyn never appeared, although the jarvey waited about for half an hour beyond the appointed time. And, as I said, we have other evidence which proves conclusively that Jermyn was killed that afternoon.'

'Which you don't intend to divulge,' said Anthea, accusingly.

'Not at present. Believe me, it's not a tale your father would want you to hear, and I must sometimes respect his wishes. Now, pray don't take a pet, for I need your help, believe me.'

'You think that the modiste's workpeople may have had a hand in the murder, do you?' asked Lady Quainton.

'You have me there. I know for certain that the man we are seeking could not himself have been the murderer, though he had some part to play. And most of the staff are females, of course.'

Anthea had been thinking. 'This means, does it not, that Sir Aubrey must have been murdered at some time after Lady St Clare left him, but before four o'clock? I see what it is, Justin, we need to know precisely when she quitted the premises! Shall one of us ask her, or will you put the question yourself to Madame Yvonne?'

'Pray consider, my dear,' objected Cassandra Quainton, 'what a prodigiously singular question it would be to ask of Stella St Clare!'

'I believe that part of the investigation will be best undertaken by Watts,' put in Justin. 'No need to put on a Friday face, Anthea, for indeed, your assistance has been invaluable.'

'Flatterer! But I'd like to do something more to help matters forward,' replied she, with a pout.

'So you shall. You say you saw Miss Jermyn and her aunt this morning? Was Lady Jermyn a little recovered, do you think?'

'I thought her almost completely restored to her normal self,' answered Lady Quainton. 'Of course, she has sustained an unpleasant shock, besides the natural grief of a bereavement. But when all's said, she and Jermyn were never close, so I think a little time will remove the melancholy impressions which now oppress her. She was quite well aware of his infidelities, you know, and realised – poor soul – that she counted for very little in his life. The unpleasantness surrounding his death may be more of a tribulation to her than the actual bereavement. I speak plain, but you would wish me to do so.'

Justin nodded.

'But he would greatly prefer to have news of Charlotte,' said Anthea, archly. 'She was looking delightfully, dear Uncle, even though she was in her blacks. Fortunately, black is becoming to her. I must tell you what she said, by the way, though I'm sorry to be obliged to admit that she didn't mention your name once.'

Justin bore this with fortitude; and presently he learned all that had passed early that morning between Lady Jermyn and Charlotte concerning Mr Leasowe's letter.

'Charlotte and I strolled about for a while on our own, so she was able to speak freely,' Anthea concluded. 'What's your opinion of all this, Justin? Do you believe that Lottie's uncle was pressing the match with Lord Escott to provide for her future? Or do you think he did indeed have some reason to fear that odious monster? For my part, I favour the latter – I don't at all see Sir Aubrey in the light of a loving, caring guardian!'

'Howsoever that may be,' pronounced Justin, 'one conclusion seems reasonable. Since Escott desired to wed Miss Jermyn, it would hardly be to his advantage to do away with her uncle, who was willing to promote the match. Little as one likes the man, it seems we must look elsewhere for the assassin.'

CHAPTER XI

The setting sun had cast a rippling track of gold across the grey blue of the sea when a smart curricle with yellow wheels pulled up outside the Old Ship inn.

The gentleman driving it tossed the reins to the groom sitting beside him, and jumped down.

'Not bad time, eh, Bowker? Might have done it in a half-hour less if they'd given us a really sweet going pair at that last change. Still, can't complain.'

'Beggin' y'r pardon, sir, but gawd 'elp us if they had!' replied the groom fervently. He was a middle-aged man who had seen some service in Viscount Rutherford's stables, and was not quite accustomed to the neck-or-nothing driving favoured on occasions by the Viscount's youngest brother.

Justin grinned. 'Thanks for the vote of confidence, Bowker. Well, we're both pretty sharp set, so stow away the curricle on the instant, there's a good chap, then drop my portmanteau into the hall on your way to the kitchen.'

He forthwith strolled into the inn with a jaunty step, and bespoke accommodation overnight for himself and the groom.

His man Selby had made the usual protest at being left behind on this expedition.

'It ill consorts with your dignity, sir,' he pointed out, in an injured tone, 'to be obliged to arrange in person for your accommodation and to order your own dinner, not to mention your being without my services in the matter of changing your attire.'

'Gammon, my dear chap,' replied Justin, cheerfully. 'My dignity must endeavour to survive a trifle of rough handling! It's only for one night, y'know.'

The landlord soon arranged matters, and Justin turned to follow one of the waiters upstairs to his rooms. As he reached the foot of the staircase, a gentleman came dashing down and almost cannoned into him.

'I say – devilish sorry, my dear sir!' he began. Then, staring hard at Justin, he exclaimed: 'B'God, Rutherford! My dear chap, I haven't run across you this age! Where have you been hiding yourself? Devilish glad to see you!'

He extended his hand, which Justin clasped cordially. He was about Justin's own years, of medium height and broad shouldered, with an open friendly countenance, keen grey eyes and auburn hair. His blue coat was from the fashionable tailor Weston and his yellow trousers fitted like a glove, but his air was not dandified. The two had been at school and Oxford together and had maintained an intermittent but firm friendship ever since.

'Glad to see you, too, Sprog! I've been here and there, y'know. Tell you about it, if you've time. Are you engaged for this evening?'

Sidney Paul Rogers grinned on hearing his schoolboy nickname, and consulted his watch.

'Said I'd look in at Raggett's club on the Steine later on, but no hurry. Have you dined, old fellow?'

'I've but this moment arrived here after tooling my curricle from London, so you may hazard a guess that I'm devilish sharp set,' returned Justin.

'Then join me when you've washed off your dirt,' invited Sprog. 'Room number six, first landing. Say in half an hour?'

Justin agreed, and found his own room.

Presently they were seated opposite each other across an amply spread board, with covers on the hot dishes. The waiter filled their glasses with claret, then withdrew.

'Here's to you, Justin,' said Sprog, raising his glass. 'Staying long? Hope so.'

Justin returned the toast. 'Only here overnight this time, regret, old chap. You staying for the season?'

The other shrugged. 'Until I'm bored with it. What are you doing here, then? Come to brood on Bodiam, or authenticate the legend of Devil's Dyke? I know well enough what queer starts you get up to.'

'You could say that,' replied Justin, reflectively, 'with some justification. I am here to look into certain matters, it's true, that go back into the past, but not so far back as Bodiam Castle – what a picture the place presents, incidentally!'

'Most romantic,' agreed Mr Rogers. 'But pray don't whet my curiosity unless you mean to satisfy it – my medico says it's bad for my constitution.'

'Gammon – you've the constitution of an ox, old fellow. All the same, perhaps I will enlighten you somewhat anent my researches. Strictly *sub rosa*, of course.'

'Silent as the grave,' promised Rogers, solemnly, refilling his guest's glass.

'More of an apt metaphor than you know. Have you heard anything of the demise of Sir Aubrey Jermyn?'

'Yes, b'Jove! Murder, wasn't it? Saw it in *The Times* a few days ago. Bit of a mystery, what? D'you know more about it, by any chance?'

'More, but not yet enough. I'm here in the hope of filling in some of the gaps in my information.'

Rogers stared at him for a moment, then snapped his fingers in a gesture of comprehension.

'Got it! That affair with Velmond, not long since!

You're playing detective again – but why? Jermyn ain't likely to have been a friend of yours, any more than he was of mine. I'll wager there's a female in it – pretty daughter?'

'Niece,' Justin corrected him, with a grin. 'How melancholy that you should read me like a book! You haven't forgotten how to read books, I trust?' he added, anxiously.

Rogers treated this remark with the contempt it deserved, and pressed for details. Justin obliged with a succinct résumé of the affair.

'So I've come here,' he concluded, 'to try and discover what happened in Brighton between these characters – Jermyn, Escott and the female who calls herself Madame Yvonne – some twenty or so years ago, before Jermyn's marriage. Can you think of anyone likely to assist me?'

Rogers drew down his tawny brows in a frown.

'You need someone who's been in residence, not a seasonal visitor,' he decided, at length. 'Most of 'em dead by now, shouldn't wonder – twenty years, I ask you! We were both scrubby schoolboys up to all kinds of high jinks at that time. So, who is there? Prinney ain't here yet, or some of his cronies might help – but Jermyn himself was one of 'em, wasn't he? Mightn't be tactful.'

'No,' agreed Justin. 'And at present I've no wish to make a stir. Tell you what, Sprog, this female Yvonne is said to be a French émigrée, possibly of aristocratic birth. That's as may be, though she don't give one that impression. But there may be something in the notion that she came originally from France. D'you chance to know any elderly Frogs, male or female, who fled here from the Revolution and are still living in the town?'

There was another pause while Rogers bent his by no means inconsiderable intellect to the question.

'Not to say know, old chap, but there is a small circle of émigrés who still keep together even after all these years. Meet 'em in Raggett's, in Donaldson's library, at the July races, and so on. Know 'em by sight.' He reflected. 'Shouldn't find it too difficult to get an introduction. Come to think of it, Beaton would do it – he plays cards with a couple of 'em sometimes. M'sister's husband, Beaton – dead bore, but we don't need to get too involved with him. They've got a house on the Marine Parade and come down every year for the season, but m'sister Fanny knows better than to expect me to dance attendance there.'

'Splendid – I knew I could reply upon you. Only trouble is, shortage of time. I plan to return late tomorrow. Events await me in London.'

'Tell you what. Have another helping of this meringue stuff – '

'If that's what you mean to tell me, I don't think much of it. No, thank you, I've had an ample sufficiency.'

'Idiot,' replied Sprog, lifting the bottle. 'Another glass, then? No, what I meant to say was – why don't we both look in at Raggett's? Beaton's sure to be there, possibly some of the Frogs, too.'

This was agreed upon; and just after ten o'clock the pair strolled up the Steine to the well-known club. Recognising Mr Rogers, the porter came forward to relieve the gentlemen of their hats, canes and gloves. They passed into the general club room, where several people greeted Rogers and were presented to his friend.

'Care for a game?' asked one. 'Easily make up a four, if you've a mind.'

Rogers thanked him, but indicated that they might not be staying.

'Seen Beaton here, by any chance?' he added. 'I wanted a word with him.'

'He's in the card room, playing piquet with another man – forget who,' was the casual reply.

Rogers nodded his thanks and guided Justin into the room beyond. Here card tables were set out and players gathered round them, a dedicated look on their faces.

'Rumour has it that a man once staked £40,000 here on a single throw of the dice,' remarked Justin. 'Must warn you that I don't aspire to anything of the kind.'

'Quite agree,' replied Rogers, casting a look around the room. 'Ah, there's Beaton.'

He moved towards a table in the far corner and Justin followed.

Two men were seated there, obviously intent upon their game. One was dark, stockily built, with thinning hair carefully arranged in an attempt to conceal the fact, and a bovine cast of countenance. He looked up as the other two appeared, a slight frown creasing his brow, then nodded.

'Evening, Rogers,' he muttered ungraciously.

His partner, an elderly gentleman, thin to the point of emaciation but elegantly attired in black coat and knee breeches with snowy linen and an intricately tied cravat, laid down his cards and, rising to his feet, bowed.

'No need of punctilio, de Valemy,' grunted Beaton, inspecting his hand by way of a hint that he did not favour interruptions. 'Only my brother-in-law and a friend of his – dare say they don't wish to stay, seeing we're engaged.'

'May I at least know to whom I have the honour of speaking?' asked the Frenchman, in silky reproof.

Beaton threw down his hand and rose to his feet.

'Monsieur de Valemy, may I present Mr Rogers,' he said, in a formal tone. 'And Mr – ?'

Justin bowed. 'Rutherford. How d'ye do?' he responded pleasantly. 'Pray don't let us interrupt your game.'

'Enchanted, gentlemen.' The Frenchman's voice was welcoming. 'We have but this hand to complete the rubber, and then would be happy to join you.'

Beaton glared, but thought it impolitic to argue. After all, his companion was winning handsomely.

'Splendid,' said Rogers. 'We'll await you in the other room.'

They strolled back, seated themselves in an alcove where four could be accommodated, and waited patiently.

'If you can draw your brother-in-law's fire,' said Justin, 'I'd like to have a *tête-à-tête* with Monsieur de Valemy.'

Rogers pursed his lips. 'Not easy. We've nothing to say to each other at the best of times – dull dog, as I warned you. Still, I'll do my possible.'

He was as good as his word when presently they were joined by the others; even managing to lead Beaton off in search of some acquaintance who could prove a point in an absurd tale with which he had begun to entertain his slow-witted brother-in-law.

Monsieur de Valemy seemed scarcely to notice their departure, so engrossed was he in the conversation of his new acquaintance. Having quickly discovered that the Frenchman had originally come from the region around Vannes, Justin spoke of his own recent visit to Brittany; of the lovely mediaeval walled town of Guerande and the impressive standing stones at Carnac, which he had especially wished to visit.

'Ah, monsieur, you interest yourself in the memorials of the past,' he said.

Somehow or other, they had slipped into speaking French, a language in which Justin was at home. It had the added advantage, he reflected, of keeping their conversation more private.

'Yes, indeed, that is my chief preoccupation. But tell me, monsieur, do you not ever wish to return to the country of your origin?'

The Frenchman shrugged, a very Gallic gesture.

'But why? All is changed there from when I was young. Besides, I've become accustomed to Brighton, and have a small circle of compatriots to keep me content. And you all, your countrymen, have been most amiable. One cannot turn back the clock. I have been here for three and twenty years, long enough to regard it almost as my own country.'

'That is fortunate. Doubtless it's true of many émigrés who arrived on these shores in 1793 or '94. Speaking of that, I wonder, monsieur, if you can possibly assist me in tracing back to her origins a female reputed to be a Frenchwoman, who is said to have arrived in Brighton at that time? I judge she would then have been in her early twenties. Unfortunately, I cannot put a name to her. She is at present know as Madame Yvonne, and keeps a fashionable gown shop in London.'

De Valemy pursed up his lips consideringly.

'There were one or two young females among those who escaped here from the Revolution. I believe they later moved away from this town, some to relatives, some to get married. For some time, one was in a state of confusion, only conscious – alas! – of one's own difficulties, paying little heed to what occurred to others.'

'This young female did stay here for several years, as I understand. She was concerned in some way with an Englishman named Jermyn whose family home, Wynsfield, is situated about five miles distant.'

'Ah! I do recollect hearing something, monsieur, but it is so long ago, and gossip was never my forte.'

'Of course not. I apologise for troubling you,' replied Justin, hiding his disappointment manfully.

'*Pas du tout*! I will help you if I can. There is a lady of my acquaintance, Madame Begard, whom I'm sure will know all about it. She is familiar with all the *on dits* both of yesterday and today.' He chuckled reminiscently.

'You are too good, monsieur. Would it be at all possible to present me to this lady? Unfortunately, I must leave for

London tomorrow – an urgent matter of business – but if I could perhaps beg a few moments of her time in the morning, before I depart? It is asking a vast deal, I realise, on so short an acquaintance.'

Seduced by this diffident appeal, Monsieur de Valemy undertook to conduct his new friend to the house of Madame Begard at a suitable hour on the following morning. Justin was well content.

Charlotte sat beside her aunt, hands demurely folded in her lap, her blue eyes covertly studying the young gentleman whom Mr Leasowe, the lawyer, had presented to them as Sir George Jermyn.

He was in his early twenties, of fair complexion and not unpleasing features, with a slight resemblance to the dead Sir Aubrey. His address was good, yet there was about him a faint air of superciliousness which brought a little frown to Charlotte's forehead. His conduct towards his bereaved relatives had been all that was proper, however, so she reproached herself for giving way to an unfavourable prejudice.

Mr Leasowe had a long, thin, countenance that matched a precise manner suited to his occupation; but, if one looked closely, his spectacles barely concealed an unexpected humorous twinkle in his eye. These same spectacles had slipped down his nose at present, as he leaned forward, reading aloud from the document before him.

'I trust that is quite clear?' he asked, looked round the intent faces before him. 'The entail is applicable only to the house in Sussex, together with the land and building thereupon and the rents thereof. That is now the property of Sir George.'

He inclined his head towards the new baronet.

'However,' he resumed, pushing his spectacles up his

sharp nose, 'the *personal* property of your late husband, ma'am, comes to you. That is to say, this house and whatever financial assets remain. Your niece, of course, has an independence settled upon her by her deceased father. But you will both – ' he bestowed a kindly twinkle on the two ladies – 'already be aware of that.'

'No,' said Charlotte, flatly.

Lady Jermyn also shook her head.

The lawyer raised his brows, then glanced at Sir George.

'I believe, sir, we need no longer detain you,' he said, in his dry tones. 'I must explain matters to these ladies, it seems, and – ahem! – sometimes with the fair sex that can be a lengthy business.'

Sir George took the hint, and rose to depart.

'I will wait upon you very soon, ladies,' he promised, 'to receive your commands anent the bestowal of any personal trifles which you may have left at Wynsfield. Your servant, ma'am – Miss Charlotte.'

His bow was exactly correct – gracious, yet dignified.

'What a very proper young man it is!' exclaimed Charlotte, scornfully, when he had gone.

'A trifle too – ? Ah, yes,' replied Mr Leasowe, twinkling again.

He shuffled the papers before him, and his expression became more serious.

'I may say at once that you need have no fears of financial embarrassment or having to make retrenchments that would be distasteful to you,' he began. 'Come, I've a wife and daughters of my own, and I'll endeavour to put it all in terms you'll readily comprehend. The country house and the rents accruing from it are gone, but so is the expense of maintenance. Gone, too, the expenses which naturally fall to a gentleman who needs to keep up his position in society. With what is left, you will be able to live here in Curzon Street in the style to which you have been accustomed. You may perhaps wish to sell off some of Sir Aubrey's blood cattle, as you'll scarce wish to go in for racing yourself, I imagine, ma'am? No, I thought not. I myself will attend to that for you. Otherwise, there need be no change in your style of living.'

'What is it, sir, about my independence?' asked Charlotte.

'Your father left you a sum of money which was invested in Consols, and which now amounts to £10,000,' replied the lawyer. 'It would have been more, but your uncle found it necessary to withdraw a certain amount to provide for your education, and for your personal allowance since leaving school.'

Lady Jermyn flushed bright scarlet.

'Well! Of all things! As if we might not have provided for the child ourselves! Indeed, I always supposed that we were doing so – had I been consulted, I would never have sanctioned any charge on her fortune, poor love!'

Mr Leasowe coughed. 'It was naturally all conducted in a proper and correct manner. Sir Aubrey was sole executor of his brother's will, but consulted me throughout. I, of course, could not prevent him from acting as he thought fit.'

'Well, I have a fortune of £10,000,' said Charlotte, brightly. 'It's respectable enough, dear Aunt Amelia, though it may not tempt the most ambitious fortune hunters, so pray don't fret.'

The lawyer regarded her approvingly. 'That's a very sensible attitude, if I may say so, Miss Charlotte. So you see, what I told you both in the beginning is quite true – you will hardly notice any diminution in your income, and may continue to live in much the same style, except that you'll no longer have a house in the country in which to pass the summer. If you wish, I might arrange for a superior lodging, say at Brighton or East Bourne, to supply that need. You have only to command me.'

They began to talk animatedly about this scheme. Presently he interrupted them with another dry cough.

'There is one other matter which I must mention. I confess I do not perfectly understand it myself, for Sir Aubrey never mentioned it to me. There is a document here – ' he tapped the papers on the table – 'which refers to the income from some kind of business concern owned jointly by Sir Aubrey and Lord Escott. The document is properly attested – though not by me – and provides that in the event of the death of either party, said income shall revert *in toto* to the second party.'

He looked up to meet two pairs of astonished eyes.

'I see you knew nothing of this, ma'am. I've made some inquiries at the bank, and the figures concerned are considerable. Rest assured, nevertheless, that your financial position is secure, even though that additional income would have made you an extremely wealthy woman.'

'Business concern?' queried Charlotte, puzzled. 'And with my Lord Escott? What can it be, sir?'

He shook his head and once more pushed his spectacles up his nose, thus effectively concealing his expression.

'My dear young lady,' he replied, quietly, 'I cannot say.'

CHAPTER XII

'But I believe he could,' said Charlotte, shrewdly, after he had taken his leave. 'For some reason, he didn't choose to do so. I wonder, you know, Aunt, whether Mr Rutherford – ' her cheeks became tinged with pink at the mention of this name, so she hurried on with what she was saying – 'might not succeed in drawing it out of him? It's several days since we saw Mr Rutherford, and we have much to tell him that may perhaps help in his task of discovering Uncle's murder.'

Lady Jermyn gave a faint shudder. 'I suppose we must offer every assistance, since he is so good as to undertake so distasteful a task. But I don't truly perceive, my dear Lottie, what fresh information we possess that could possibly be of value.'

'Why, what Mr Leasowe has this minute told us, about my uncle and Lord Escott being engaged in some form of business enterprise together! I mentioned to Anthea yesterday, when we met in the Park, that you and I had been discussing some such possibility. And you may be sure that she has already passed that on to Mr Rutherford. Now we can confirm it, and perhaps he'll be able to discover exactly what the nature of this business may be.'

'I don't quite see how it will benefit us to know. If Mr Leasowe had thought it important, be sure he would have told us.'

'But – ' Charlotte halted, struck by the logic of this. 'I suppose you are right,' she allowed, weakly. 'I must admit that it's only curiosity on my part, and may have nothing whatever to do with – with my uncle's demise. Unless – ' She broke off, pondering.

'Unless what, my love?' asked Lady Jermyn.

'Oh, nothing,' replied Charlotte, hurriedly. 'But all the same, I think we should talk with Mr Rutherford, if only to learn what progress has been made.'

Her aunt glanced at her with a faint smile.

'Since you think so, then by all means let me arrange a meeting, Lottie. Why not send round a note to Anthea suggesting that she might call here with Mr Rutherford, should he be able to spare us a few moments of his time? Nothing too urgent and encroaching, of course – but I know I may safely leave it to your discretion.'

Charlotte's eyes became more strikingly blue all at once, and she rose quickly to carry out this welcome suggestion. But at that moment, another visitor was announced, and Lord Escott walked into the room.

He looked very elegant in his well-cut dark blue coat, fawn trousers and glossy Hessians. Lady Jermyn had to acknowledge that he certainly had an air.

They greeted him politely, offered refreshment which he refused equally politely, and begged him to be seated.

'I am come to offer my condolences to you both, ma'am,' he said, with a slightly sardonic expression. 'A trifle belatedly, perhaps, but I judged that an interval of time was needed for you to recover from the first shock of such a sad loss.'

'You are very good, my lord,' replied Lady Jermyn, with as much warmth as she could master for a man whom she never liked. 'In truth, it is but during the last few days that I have felt myself sufficiently recovered to be receiving visits of condolence.'

'So I collect, ma'am, and therefore decided that I might now venture to present myself, not wishing to be behind hand in any attention. I take it that so far the authorities haven't yet brought to account the perpetrator of this foul deed?'

'Not as far as we know,' replied Charlotte. 'Though we are fortunate enough not to be obliged to see them always on our doorstep, since we have a kind intermediary to act for us.'

Escott smiled in a sneering fashion. 'Ah, yes, the indefatiguable Justin Rutherford, a young man whose odd taste it is to meddle in such – ah – unpleasant matters. I had the doubtful felicity of an interview with him at the start of this unfortunate affair, when it was yet assumed that Jermyn was merely missing for a brief spell.'

Indignation brought the colour to Charlotte's cheeks.

'My aunt and I are prodigiously grateful to Mr Rutherford for his generous assistance.'

The sneer became more pronounced.

'Doubtless he knows how to recommend himself to the fair sex. I have heard something of the kind rumoured – though, of course, one never heeds idle gossip. But I believe you have an excellent lawyer who could perform the same office?'

Lady Jermyn herself answered this time.

'Perhaps so, sir. But in the beginning, I was anxious not to make any kind of stir, and lawyers *do* work through official channels, as you know. Mr Leasowe would have recommended me to go to Bow Street, which at that time was the last thing I desired.' She sighed unhappily. 'Now, alas – '

'There is no choice,' he finished for her. 'The story is that the – ah – murder was committed somewhere in the vicinity of Guy's hospital. Have either the Bow Street Runners or the worthy Rutherford succeeded in discovering precisely where and when, as yet?'

'I was talking to Anthea Rutherford only yesterday,' replied Charlotte, 'and she had nothing to report on that head.'

This was quite true, as when they had met in the Park Anthea had not yet seen Justin and heard of his suspicions; but Charlotte had no intention of sharing even the little she did know with Lord Escott.

'And of course that ebullient young lady will certainly be on confidential terms with Rutherford,' said Escott, with a twist of his thin lips. 'Her *uncle* – is it not absurd? So I take it that nothing further has been discovered? I fear it's a mystery that's destined to remain unsolved.'

His tone nettled Charlotte to the degree that she was betrayed into saying something indiscreet.

'There is another mystery which our lawyer Mr Leasowe presented to us, this morning, my lord. He told us of a business agreement existing between my uncle and yourself, but couldn't enlighten us as to what kind of business it was, since he had not been called in to do the legal work. Perhaps you can give us that information?'

He smiled, but his eyes were hostile.

'Ah, but I never discuss business with ladies, Miss Charlotte. In all else, I am yours to command. Should your man of business – Leasowe, did you say? – wish to look into the matter with my own lawyer, he is naturally totally at liberty to do so. Pray refer him to me.'

She bowed curtly, conscious of having allowed him to score a point.

There was a short pause, during which Lady Jermyn tried in vain to find something to say. At last, he rose.

'Obviously this is not the time,' he said, smoothly, 'for me to renew my addresses to you, Miss Charlotte. I would like you to know that my unswerving devotion is yours, and to remember that your deceased relative strongly supported my claim on your interest. There may unfortunately be a deal of scandal bruited abroad before this affair is done. You may be glad to shelter beneath the protection of my name.'

'I thank you, my lord,' she said, stiffly, as she rose to ring for the footman to show him out. 'I think you already know my sentiments. They are not likely to change.'

He bowed and took his leave.

'The devil of it is,' said Rupert Blake to his sister, 'that now Charlotte Jermyn is in mourning – officially, at any rate, for I'm cursed sure she never cared a rush for that uncle of hers! – there's no coming near her. She don't go to any of the balls and parties, nor go riding in the Park, and a fellow don't care to call round there too often, for fear of upsetting Lady J.'

'No, it is difficult,' agreed Mary. 'But one must observe the conventions, after all.'

'A fig for the conventions!' snapped her brother. 'How am I supposed to pay my attentions? I did think that once that black hearted, loose fish of an uncle was removed, my way might be clear. Mean to say, while he was alive I knew he'd never consent to a match between us – too set on keeping in with Escott. I tell you it's an outrage to think of that depraved old roué in connection with anyone as sweet and innocent as Miss Jermyn! But one consolation is that this will have put a spoke in his wheel, too, for he won't be able to press his suit during the mourning period, thank God! any more than I can. I hadn't thought of that.'

Mary Blake listened to this speech with some misgiving.

'I do trust, Rupert, that you'll have a care not to talk in that style in front of anyone else. People might well suppose that you had something to do with Sir Aubrey's murder.'

'D'you think I'm an idiot, girl? It's a poor thing if I can't speak plain to my own sister, but I'm not such a nodcock as to shoot off my mouth to anyone else. That reminds me – that fellow Rutherford we saw at the Jermyns the other day. D'you suppose he's hanging out after Miss Jermyn, too?'

Miss Blake considered this. 'Well, there was certainly some pretty by-play between them,' she said at last, with a teasing smile.

He scowled. 'Yes, damn him, I observed that! For two pins, I'd make him pay for that piece of impudence, too!'

'For heavens' sake, don't be so hasty, Rupert! You can't call anyone out, in this present time, for such things belong to our parents' generation, and would not only be considered bad *ton*, but – what is worse – ludicrous. And fisticuffs are the resort of schoolboys! Besides, I do believe – ' she paused, reflecting for a moment – 'that he was only baiting you, and it was just a piece of nonsense.'

'Hell and the devil! D'you suppose it turns me up sweet to be told that? Evidently the fellow takes me for some sort of maudlin idiot – I tell you, I'll not tolerate it!'

She placed a restraining hand upon his arm.

'Pray don't do anything impetuous, Rupert. Try and think before you act, or you may find yourself in trouble.'

'Bah, what trouble?'

He spoke contemptuously, but his glance was tolerant enough, for he knew she had his welfare at heart.

'I don't quite know,' she said, slowly, 'but I believe that the murder of Sir Aubrey Jermyn is no ordinary matter – that's to say, it was not the work of footpads or commonplace criminals. That being so, the Bow Street Runners may be looking for those who might have been his enemies. You must be on your guard.'

'Good God, what a girl you are for thinking up alarums! As if Bow Street would think of suspecting the *ton* of a felony – besides, they're a set of stupid addlepates, in any event.'

'Don't be too certain of that. They are asking questions here and there, and it would be as well if you had some answers ready, lest they chance to approach you. Your quarrel with Sir Aubrey over his refusal to allow you to pay your addresses to Charlotte is bound to have been made the subject of gossip, though naturally *we* would not hear it.'

His brow darkened as he recalled the scene.

'For instance,' continued Mary, 'what were you doing on the day he disappeared? Everyone now knows that he didn't go off to his estate in Sussex, although Lady Jermyn gave that explanation at first, thinking to silence idle tongues.'

'B'God, you seem vastly well informed, sister!'

She shrugged. 'I merely attend to the gossip that's circulating. You must have heard it at the Clubs. But can you recall what you were doing that day?'

'Damme, how can I, when I'm not even certain what day it was?'

'It was close on a fortnight since – the Monday before last,' she informed him.

He frowned irritably. 'Who can say, at this distance in time? All the usual things, I suppose – the Clubs, Tattersall's, riding in the Park – who's to say?'

'Well, at least *I* can say what you were doing in the afternoon, just after four o'clock, for we chanced to encounter each other as I was coming out of Madame Yvonne's shop. You told me you'd been in Bond Street for several hours at Jackson's boxing saloon there, and we walked home together.'

'Did we, b'God? What a girl you are for unimportant detail, ain't you? Can't say I recollect that particular occasion, but then I'm often at Gentleman Jackson's saloon.'

'It may not be so unimportant,' she said, in a warning tone. 'In fact, you'd be wise to try and piece together what you did with the rest of that day. And pray, brother, do endeavour to keep a guard upon your tongue.'

It was close on seven o'clock when Justin, somewhat travel-stained and decidedly sharp set, arrived back in Albemarle Street from Brighton.

The admirable Selby greeted him with sensible suggestions for a nourishing meal which could be quickly prepared while his master was sluicing off the dust of the roads and changing his dress.

'Splendid,' approved Justin. 'I'll leave it to you. What's this, Selby?'

The manservant had handed him a note.

'It was left by Miss Rutherford, who called this afternoon and was sorry to learn that you were in Brighton. She wrote the note at your desk, and particularly requested me to hand it to you as soon as you arrived home. Otherwise I should not have troubled you with it until you had dined, sir.'

Justin unfolded the note and quickly scanned its contents.

You will be delighted to learn, dear Uncle, that Charlotte Jermyn is to dine with us this evening, and particularly desires your presence. Selby tells me that you are gone to Brighton and cannot say when you may return. If at any time before eleven o'clock, pray join us, for I believe you will find it rewarding! If you do not return until tomorrow, however, you will miss a heaven-sent opportunity of gazing into those cerulean blue eyes! In which case, I weep for you.

Your dutiful niece,

Anthea

He thrust the note into his pocket.

'No need to trouble with any provender, Selby, as I'm off to Lord Rutherford's house. They'll find me some bread and cheese, I dare say. Should the Runner Watts chance to call while I'm absent, offer him the usual facilities, will you? Home about midnight. Oh, and lay out my evening dress rig, please.'

'I was about to do so, sir,' replied Selby, with dignity.

'Good man – know I can rely on you.'

Barely half an hour later, he presented himself in Grosvenor Square just as the family and their guest were about to sit down to dinner.

Anthea gave him an approving glance as greetings were exchanged. Usually, he wore his clothes with a casual air; that evening, he had taken trouble, and the formal attire became him.

During the meal conversation was general, and the subject of the murder at first studiously avoided. Only once did they approach it, and then Justin steered it skilfully away. He had mentioned his lightning visit to Brighton, giving an amusing picture of the ritual daily fashion promenade round the Steine.

'Brighton, eh?' asked Edward, curiosity momentarily overcoming discretion. 'What made you go there? Anything to do with that business about Jer – that's to say,' he added, hastily, fidgeting with his wine glass – 'any particular reason?'

'Pleasant place to go at the start of the season,' replied Justin, smoothly. 'Sea breezes benefit one's health, according to the worthy Dr Russell.'

'You were scarce long enough there for a cure,' objected Lady Rutherford, with a laugh.

'True, but even a few hours may work wonders, do you not think so, Miss Jermyn?'

Blue eyes smiled into his, and his pulse momentarily quickened.

'Indeed, Brighton can be vastly stimulating, but at

times it's a trifle too breezy,' she replied. 'We go there every year – '

She broke off, recollecting that things were different now.

'But now that Wynsfield is no longer ours,' she continued, 'we perhaps may not do so. Mr Leasowe, our lawyer, did say, however, that he would look for a suitable house for us, should my aunt desire to continue passing the summer months at the seaside.'

'Wynsfield no longer yours?' queried Edward, sharply. 'What do you mean, Miss Jermyn?'

'It's entailed,' she said, simply. 'The new baronet, Sir George Jermyn, was introduced to us this morning. Mr Leasowe explained everything.'

'You did not know of this before?' asked Justin, while the others gave various exclamations of sympathy.

'We had no notion. I dare say it should have occurred to us, but it did not, and my uncle never discussed matters of the kind with Aunt Amelia. I collect that gentlemen seldom talk of business affairs with their female relatives.'

'Lord, no,' agreed Edward. 'Still, all the same – '

'I suppose Sir George Jermyn must be a distant relative,' said Anthea, 'since you've told me that your uncle had no other brothers than your father.'

Charlotte nodded. 'Yes. He's the son of my father's cousin, who died some years ago. We have never had anything to do with the family, and all my aunt and I knew of him was that my uncle had once or twice mentioned that the title would pass to him.'

'I feel for Lady Jermyn,' said Elizabeth Rutherford. 'It must be melancholy indeed to lose a house that has been in the family for generations.'

'But not in my aunt's family, ma'am,' put in Charlotte, quickly. 'She came to Wynsfield as a bride, and I don't believe ever became attached to it, for she was quite happy to live in London for the better part of the year, which was my uncle's preference.'

'And you?' queried Lord Rutherford.

Charlotte shrugged. 'I'm quite content with the town house. All my friends are in London, after all. And since we are not to become paupers, which I'll own might have been odious, my aunt and I are agreed we shall go on tolerably well.'

Justin deftly changed the subject. Dinner proceeded, and when it was over, the ladies as usual retired to the drawing room for a while. Anthea would have dearly liked to find out more about the new baronet from her friend; but even she knew better than to introduce such a topic before her mama, whose notions of propriety would have been offended. She had been sadly put out by Lady Jermyn's polite but firm refusal to accompany Charlotte this evening. Mama and Charlotte's aunt could then have chatted together, while the two girls enjoyed a tête-à-tête on their own. But Lady Jermyn's own sense of propriety forbade her acceptance of dinner invitations so soon after her husband's demise. Anthea sighed; truly, the older generation could be a monstrous trial at times.

She did manage, however, to manoeuvre matters so that Justin was seated beside Charlotte on the sofa when the gentlemen joined the ladies. It gave her great satisfaction, and some amusement, to watch them in earnest conversation for at least ten minutes, until civility required them to give their attention to the company in general.

The conversation, however, was not entirely taken up with the exchanges usual between a male and female who are mutually attracted. Charlotte seized the opportunity to inform Justin of the mystery concerning Lord Escott's business partnership with her uncle.

'Certainly the terms of the contract are unusual,' said Justin. 'Do you think Lady Jermyn would have any objection if I had a word with your lawyer on this subject?'

'I know she would not, sir, for we've already discussed the possibility.' She hesitated. 'You see, I felt that when Mr Leasowe told us he didn't know what manner of business it was, he was not being entirely frank. And it did occur to me that he would perhaps have been more open with a gentleman, rather than with females.'

'I see. What conclusions did you draw from that, Miss Jermyn?'

'Oh, I don't know. It was just a fleeting impression, you understand – dare I say feminine intuition?' She flashed her devastating smile on him. 'But I'll admit that I'm not in general guided by such an irrational impulse, which I know is mocked at by gentlemen.'

'Falsely, if indeed it is. Intuition is merely the result of an unconscious thought process relying on the evidence of one's senses. It's used by both sexes.'

'How very kind of you to make it sound respectable! Now I can be easy again!'

He smiled down into her eyes.

'You're bamming me, ma'am! I don't believe you ever knew a moment's uneasiness about your use of that hackneyed expression. Your real object is to expose me for a prosy fellow.'

'Indeed I wouldn't be so ungrateful!' she began, indignantly.

They both burst into laughter.

'I take the point, ma'am. Prosy I may be, but gratitude seals your lips!'

'You're a vast deal too bad, sir,' she replied, sternly, 'twisting everything I say in that odious manner!'

'Come, this is better. We shall go on tolerably well if you berate me now and then, whenever I appear to be getting above myself.'

She shook her head at him, her pert little nose in the air.

'You are indeed a sad case. But seriously, Mr Rutherford, are you any closer to a solution of the mystery? Anthea has acquainted me with the whole, and I suppose I ought to say that I was very much shocked to learn of my uncle's assignations – but honesty compels me to admit that I was not at all surprised. I have been wondering, you know – ' she lowered her voice – 'if Lord Pryme could have had anything to do with it? And then again, since Lord Escott knew he would be the beneficiary of that business agreement – ' She broke off; and at that juncture they were both drawn into the general conversation.

After the tea tray was brought in, Charlotte soon departed. This time, Justin did not kiss her hand; but held it a fraction longer than courtesy required, while they exchanged warm glances.

He himself left not long afterwards, promising Anthea *sotto voce* that he would keep her informed of events and allow her, as she put it, to join in the fun.

He reached home to find Watts awaiting him. The Runner had been there only half an hour, and had been provided with a tankard of ale by the thoughtful Selby. He leapt to his feet as Justin entered.

'How d'ye do?' the latter greeted him. 'You bring news, I trust.'

'Aye, sir, good news. We've arrested Carter – found him in the warrens around St Giles – and he's been questioned. D'ye know what? He states that deceased was buried by him and his mates on the orders of that Madame Yvonne!'

CHAPTER XIII

'I think,' said Justin, 'we would like to hear your account of what occurred here on the day of Sir Aubrey Jermyn's death, before we ask you to accompany us to Bow Street.'

They were facing Madame Yvonne in that same private parlour where Jermyn had been observed by Anthea almost a fortnight since. Justin had entered the salon while Watts had gone round to the private entrance in the side street. All had been managed quietly; Justin had conveyed to the proprietress the confidential nature of their visit, and she had admitted them both to this room.

She began to deny once again that Jermyn had ever been on her premises, but Watts cut her short.

'That tale won't fadge, Madam, on account of the man Carter's under arrest and has told us different. What's more, his accomplices have confessed to assisting him in the disposal of the body upon your orders. The girl Bates has been questioned, too, and she confirms this.'

Madame Yvonne's face, usually aloof and controlled, crumpled all at once. She groped her way unseeingly to the nearest chair and collapsed into it. For a few moments, she said nothing, staring blankly before her.

'Shall I begin the story at the beginning?' asked Justin, quietly.

She spoke then. 'What do you know?'

'That your name is Mademoiselle Yvonne Rochet,' he

replied, in the same unemphatic tone. 'You arrived in England in 1793 together with your mistress, the Comtesse de Vailly, fleeing from the Revolution. You were then two and twenty, and, as I understand, a very attractive young woman.'

Her mouth twisted wryly.

'*Merci du compliment!*'

'Your mistress settled in Brighton, and before long you had attracted the attention of several young bucks come there from London for the summer season. Among your admirers was one not so young – Lord Escott.'

'I see monsieur has been busying himself with my past affairs,' she said, tartly, beginning to recover.

'And most interesting I found them,' he retorted. 'When the Comtesse died some eighteen months later, you were left penniless and without a roof over your head. Who could blame an abigail in a foreign country if she had accepted the protection of a man to whom she had already granted her favours, albeit secretly until then? But you did not do that. Instead you chose a young man of five and twenty, a devil-may-care whose name was Aubrey Jermyn, and whose family home was nearby.'

'I was foolish enough to fall in love, monsieur,' she murmured, a reminiscent gleam in her eyes. 'He was, as you say, reckless, dashing, handsome – everything, in short, that captivates a girl's heart. Beside him, milord Escott was of no account whatsoever. Jermyn offered to set me up as his mistress in a pleasant house on the Marine Parade. What would you?' She shrugged in a very Gallic gesture.

'You quickly gave Escott his congé,' continued Justin, 'thereby making a lifelong enemy for both yourself and Jermyn. A man of his stamp doesn't care to be cast aside like an old glove.'

'Well, he had his revenge soon enough, *n'est-ce pas?* Less

than two years later – in 1797 – Jermyn played the same trick.' Her mouth twisted in a long forgotten agony momentarily relived. 'He inherited the estate on his father's death, and at once informed me that he was soon to wed, so our connection must come to an end.'

Justin nodded. 'But despite your broken heart, Madame, your French practical common sense did not entirely desert you, I collect? You wheedled Jermyn – or was it stronger than that, was it blackmail? – into giving you a sum of money sufficient to enable you to start a small modiste's shop in Brighton. My female relatives inform me that you have an undoubted flair for fashion allied to a dedicated devotion to your business interests. After a few years, you transferred your activities to an unpretentious commercial quarter in London. Finally, nine years since, you attained the crux of your ambition by moving into your present highly desirable premises.'

Her mouth relaxed into a triumphant smile.

'It is true. Me, I have worked hard, and built all this –' her outflung arms embraced the whole building – 'from nothing! And so do you think I am to let anything interfere with it – anything at all? No, never, never!'

'That is what I supposed. It accounts for much,' returned Justin, cryptically. 'I think, Madame, you never wed, though after Escott and Jermyn there were other men for short periods? I think, too, that you never returned to Jermyn, even after you chanced upon each other again here in Town?'

'No. Men, bah, what use are they in the long run? I did not see that one at all from our parting in Brighton until some months after I settled here in Bond Street. Then one day we met by chance, as you say, monsieur. Jermyn had been visiting that Boxing saloon in Bond Street – you know the one? – and I was outside my shop, having just escorted a valuable client to her carriage. After a long stare at the features which time had somewhat changed, alas! we recognised each other. It was a shock, believe me.'

So that was the way of it. 'And you didn't then resume – ah – your earlier relationship?'

She shook her head with a contemptuous look.

'Me, I had had enough of men by that time, *voyez-vous*! Nothing of that kind, but he did suggest that we might be of mutual benefit, he and I. He would instruct his wife to patronise me and to recommend me to all her friends in the *ton*. In return, I was to allow him to use this private room from time to time for his secret assignations. It seemed a fair bargain, as I then needed influential custom.'

'And it was easy to arrange the meetings without involving *you* in any scandal,' put in Watts, who had been content so far to leave the interview to Justin. 'He could get into this room by your private side entrance without causing notice, while the lady came by way of the concealed door in that cubby hole in your showroom.'

'You know of that?' she asked, startled.

'We knows a deal more than ye gives us credit for, Madam. All the same, we still need to know why it was you killed this man.'

'Killed him!' shrieked Madame. 'Oh, no, no!'

'Killed him,' repeated Watts, grimly, 'or else had him killed, one or t'other. And then made arrangements for his burial. A cool hand, ye are, and no mistake! Best confess, Madam.'

'But – but – it is all a mistake!' she cried, beside herself. 'It wasn't like that, *pas du tout*! I – you – oh, dear God!'

'Brandy,' said Justin.

She gestured towards a wall cupboard, and he opened it to find bottles and glasses within. He poured a generous glass from the brandy bottle, presenting it to her. She took it in a trembling hand, quickly, gulping a third of the contents, then coughing violently for a moment.

He took the glass from her, setting it down on a small table close to her chair.

'When you are ready, Madame,' he said, in quiet tones.

She said nothing for a few moments, sipping the brandy and pulling herself together with an effort. At last she fixed them with a steady, though desperate, regard.

'I didn't kill him,' she repeated, more calmly than before. 'I found him already dead – shot through the heart – Parker will be witness to the truth of that!'

'We'll question Parker once we've done with you,' said Watts, firmly. 'Start at the beginning, Madam, and no prevarication, mind.'

She gave him a hostile look, but answered quietly enough.

'He came here to meet – a lady – as he'd arranged with me. He had his own key to the street door, but I always left it unlocked on days when I knew there was a rendezvous arranged. She – the lady – '

'Shall we give her a name?' asked Justin. 'We are aware that the lady was the Viscountess St Clare. No need to avoid it between these four walls.'

She nodded miserably. 'I see you know the whole. Very well. She entered this room by the way of which you know. She arrived at the salon about a quarter to three, though we'd been expecting her earlier. Then, about a half-hour later, a crisis arose. The Earl of Pryme – you will know he is Viscount St Clare's father? – called at the salon, saying he was come to escort his daughter-in-law home!'

'Yes, I can see that would have been awkward,' agreed Justin.

'Naturally I kept my wits about me,' she continued, in her normal tones. 'I said that the dressmaker was still giving milady a fitting, but I would send to hurry matters if he would be pleased to take a seat meanwhile. He declined, saying he would call back later.'

'So of course you sent to warn the pair,' put in Justin.

'Yes. But I went myself, for although Parker knew of the arrangement, she is an old maid, you understand, and there was no saying what she might find. Besides, she was attending to a customer.'

He nodded. 'You say Pryme arrived at about a quarter after three? I would like you to be as precise as possible about these times.'

'There's a clock on the mantleshelf in the salon, sir. I'm in the habit of consulting it frequently, since time is money, is it not? But on this occasion I had good cause, for Milord Pryme was to call back soon, and Lady St Clare must be told, so as to be ready for him.'

'So you went off to warn the lovebirds, ye say,' put in Watts. 'Which way did you go, along the passage or through the concealed door?'

'I used the concealed door – it was quicker, and, moreover, Lady St Clare would come out by that way, should anyone be noticing. I didn't wait for her, of course, after I'd delivered my warning. She came into the salon soon afterwards. I should say not more than ten minutes.'

'Which brings us to twenty-five past three,' murmured Justin. 'Who was the other customer in the showroom, Madame?'

She gave a contemptuous shrug. 'A young lady of small account, a Miss Blake, whom even I cannot dress to advantage, though one does one's poor best.'

His eyebrows shot up. 'Blake, what? Did the lady chance to be accompanied by her brother?'

'No, but she encountered Mr Blake on the pavement outside, as she left the salon. I was busy at the time, but noticed them through the window, in the way one does.'

'Would this be before or after Lord Pryme called back for his daughter-in-law?'

'Not long afterwards. Milord kept the lady waiting until

turned ten minutes to four, which was just as well. She was in a sad taking, so it gave her time to recover. There was a little bustle in the salon from about half past three – several customers, and an abigail calling here to take home a garment for her mistress. I was busy, but I did fancy once that I heard a short, sharp sound from this room. However, there was such a babble of talk going on that I paid no heed, not to mention that my mind was upon Lady St Clare's dilemma.'

'You can't positively give us a time for that?' demanded Justin, sharply. 'It might have been the shot that killed Jermyn.'

'Oh, *mon Dieu!*' she clapped her hands to her head distractedly. 'Lady St Clare had been seated in the salon, waiting, for close on quarter of an hour, I would think – though I cannot be sure, sir! I was occupied, you see, so didn't glance at the clock until Milord Pryme returned. I am sorry.'

'No matter. In any event, it may not have been that. Your times, Madame, have so far been helpful.'

She gave him a grateful look. 'If only you will believe that I didn't kill Jermyn!'

He ignored this. 'What occurred next?'

'After Lady St Clare and Milord had departed and while we were still dealing with our clients, I thought I heard a distant knocking, as it might be on the door in the side street,' she continued, anxious not to omit anything. 'Then, after my last client had gone, I came into this room, expecting that Jermyn would be gone. I found – *mon Dieu*, you know what I found!'

She had recourse to the brandy glass again.

'Can you inform us what time this was?' asked Justin gently.

She frowned in an effort of recollection.

'I cannot be sure, but it would be towards half past four,

when the salon was empty. We do not have many clients dropping in after four o'clock. It is not a fashionable hour for shopping.'

'So you found Jermyn dead – are you sure he was dead?'

'Monsieur, I saw death often in my native country when I was young – death in many forms,' she answered, grimly. 'This was a bullet wound. Oh, yes, he was quite dead.'

Justin nodded. Astley Cooper had given it as his professional opinion that the bullet would have killed instantly.

'What did you do, Madame?'

'After a few moments making sure that it was so, I began to consider. At all costs, it must not make a scandal for my establishment! And that it would do most certainly, did I inform the authorities! So – there seemed only one thing possible. I must have the corpse removed, it must be found elsewhere. But how to contrive? After a little while, I saw how.'

'Danger concentrates the mind powerfully, Madame,' remarked Justin. 'You thought of the man Carter. But tell us how you know of him?'

'I found him and that wench Bates snuggled down together in the workroom one evening after all the others had gone home. I was for dismissing her out of hand and sending for the constable to deal with him, but the hussy told me she knew all about Jermyn's assignations, and would make sure everyone else did, too, if I acted against them. The man Carter let slip that he'd no desire to see a constable as he'd been in trouble before. That was why I suddenly thought of him as someone who'd remove the body and keep his mouth shut, if I paid him enough. So I told Parker to fetch the girl, and warned them both not to set up a screech when they entered the room. I explained what I wanted to Bates, then sent her off in a hackney to summon Carter. Luckily, there was a hack outside in the side street, so no time was lost.'

Watts looked at Justin. 'That'd be our witness, guv'nor.'

Justin nodded. 'And all went as you hoped?'

'Yes. Carter came after dark with two other ruffians. They put the corpse into one of those trunks you may have noticed in the other room, and went off with it much as my delivery men take bales of cloth from time to time. If anyone observed them, nothing would be thought of it, except that they were working somewhat late. It was a sound scheme, but as you see – ' she lifted one shoulder in a fatalistic Gallic shrug – 'it has come to nothing, alas.'

'And you have no notion who could have shot Jermyn?'

'No. There are several who might wish to, and some of those were in the vicinity – but no, I cannot point to anyone in particular.'

'Some of those?' queried Justin. 'Whom did you see, Madame, besides Pryme, who might have been an enemy?'

'Escott, for example. He always bore Jermyn a grudge for the early days in Brighton, as you yourself pointed out, sir. And although of late years they were involved together in some affair of business, I know neither liked the other.'

'That may be so,' agreed Justin, reflecting that there were two other more recent motives which might have induced Escott to do away with Jermyn. 'But where and when did you see him on that day?'

'I saw him briefly when I was escorting Miss Rutherford to her carriage. He was strolling along on the opposite side of the street. As to when, I suppose it must have been close on a quarter to three. But any one of a score of cuckolded husbands might have decided to shoot Jermyn – that would not surprise one.'

'I think, though, it would surprise one that the murderer should be familiar enough with your premises to find his way to this room without being observed,' said Justin.

'I should suppose that few customers or their escorts ever venture beyond the salon and the fitting rooms?'

'True, but the workpeople might talk to an interested party for a consideration. Only think of that hussy Bates, knowing too much for her own good – and mine! As for Escott, he knew his way about here well enough, for he's made use of this room himself on a few occasions. I could not gainsay him, once he discovered Jermyn's assignations.'

'And you swear that you yourself did not shoot Jermyn?' demanded Justin, brusquely.

She jumped up in protest at this, then gave a gasp.

She found herself looking down the barrel of a pistol.

CHAPTER XIV

She put up her arms before her face in a defensive gesture.

'*Mon Dieu*! Do not shoot! What are you about?'

'Have no fear,' said Justin, quietly. 'This isn't loaded, so can do no harm. An experiment, merely.' He handed the pistol to her. 'Take it.'

She hesitated, her expression suggesting that she thought him mad.

'Come,' he urged. 'It's not loaded, I assure you. Take it in your right hand – that's the dandy, so – now level it at me, as if about to shoot me through the heart.'

Bewildered, she attempted to obey his instructions. But as soon as she raised her right arm with the pistol in her hand, it began to tremble convulsively. She brought the left hand across to try and steady it, with only limited success.

'I – I cannot,' she mumbled. 'This right arm of mine has a weakness – I cannot lift a cup or glass filled with liquid to my mouth without spilling the contents. My medical man says it's a failure of muscle control – advancing years, I suppose.'

Justin nodded, stepping forward to remove the pistol from her.

'I had observed the disability previously, Madame. It adds credence to your claim that you didn't kill Jermyn yourself. You cannot hold a pistol steady, and he was shot through the heart by a good marksman – maybe a female, but not you, I believe.'

She let out a gasp of relief.

'Thank God for that! Besides, how should I come by a pistol, here?' she added, beginning to take a calmer view. 'And he, Jermyn, would not be carrying one, considering the nature of his errand.'

'True. And now, Madame, we would like to see Miss Parker. Watts will accompany you to summon her, then you may remain in the showroom to deal with any clients who come. I need not say that you must on no account attempt to leave the premises.'

She bowed her head in acquiescence, and preceded Watts from the room.

Justin swiftly walked round, examining everything. The hidden door functioned smoothly. There was a tall cupboard against the wall, not far from the door; opening it, he disclosed nothing but a few pegs for hanging garments. He reflected, though, that it was large enough to conceal a man. The furniture was of rosewood, elegant and tasteful, but it held no surprises such as a writing desk might have offered. There was a shelf of books on one wall, some in the French language.

Miss Parker and Watts returned before he had time to do more.

The assistant was in a state so nearly approaching terror that it was difficult to get anything out of her except monosyllables at first.

Yes, she had been with Madame a long time; yes, before she came to Bond Street. No, she had not been with her in Brighton. No, she was not in partnership with Madame. Yes, it would be true to say that she identified herself very closely with her employer's business interests. Yes, she would do a great deal to prevent scandal coming near the salon.

'This is praiseworthy,' said Justin, in an encouraging tone. 'Would we could all count on such faithful servants! Now, Miss Parker, pray have no fear. As long as you tell us truthfully this time what occurred here on the day in question, we can forget that you lied to us when we questioned you before. We have been told that Madame summoned you from the salon to this room when she discovered the dead man. Was that the first time you'd set eyes on him that day?'

'Ye'd best answer truthfully, mind,' warned Watts, as she hesitated.

'Not the first time, no. I caught a glimpse of him coming in at the street door as I was about to go downstairs to the basement.'

'Can you say what o'clock it was?' asked Watts.

'Just after two, it must have been – say, ten minutes past.'

'You were aware of the arrangement between Jermyn and Madame?' put in Justin.

She nodded.

'So you didn't wonder at seeing him there? And I suppose you hastened on your way downstairs so that he might not feel himself spied upon? Very natural. How long did your errand to the basement occupy you?'

She flushed. He realised that he might have been indelicate, and felt sorry for her. He was about to say it did not matter, when she answered.

'Not more than ten mintues, for I was too late.'

Both men eyed her keenly.

'Too late for what?' demanded Watts.

'For – for – the person I'd arranged to see in the yard,' she mumbled in embarrassment.

'I think you'd better explain, Miss Parker,' suggested Justin.

'Oh, must I?'

She flushed again, looking appealingly at them. Her unfortunate resemblance to a camel somewhat spoiled the effect of this.

'Afraid so,' he insisted, quiet but firm.

'Oh, dear! It is simply that – you don't need to tell Madame Yvonne, do you? She would not at all like it, I fear, though why a female cannot be permitted – however – ' as she saw signs of impatience – 'it was a gentleman friend I had hoped to see. Only for a few minutes, to arrange another meeting after I left here in the evening. I would not dare to waste Madame's time in my private concerns! He said he would come at ten minutes before two o'clock, but I couldn't get away, you see, try as I might. And by the time I managed to escape, he had gone. There was no sign of him.'

'Hmm. Not very gallant, was it?' asked Justin.

Watts occupied himself in an effort to restrain his mirth at the thought of Miss Parker with a lovelorn swain.

'He, like myself, is not free to do as he chooses,' she replied, with a touch of her habitual loftiness. 'He is in service.'

'Have you known him long?'

She considered. 'About two months, I think. We met first at the Baptist chapel which I attend on Sundays. I hadn't seen him before in the congregation, because he was newly arrived in London. Naturally, I was not on-coming with him – I trust you don't think me that kind of female – ' the nose went up in camel style – 'but after a time I permitted him to walk me home, and for the past few weeks, we have been walking out together, whenever he can find the free time to do so. It isn't very often, so I'm sorry to have missed him on that day. I haven't seen him at all since – he's not even been in chapel. I do trust that I haven't offended him deeply by not keeping our appointment.'

Justin knew a moment's compassion. It sounded as if the unknown follower had tired of poor Miss Parker. Most likely it had no direct bearing on the murder of Jermyn; but anyone either in the vicinity at that time or expected to be so, might be of interest.

'What is your friend's name and who is his employer?'

'His name is William Trimble, but he never told me where he worked.'

'What kind of servant is he?' demanded Watts.

'That he never said, but I think he's a superior sort,' said Miss Parker, proudly. 'He speaks ever so proper, he does.'

Watts made a quick note of the name before passing to the events after Madame's discovery of Jermyn's body.

Parker's account tallied closely with that of her employer; but neither Justin nor Watts considered this conclusive. There had been plenty of time since the murder for a story to have been concocted between them.

Parker told them that Madame had been absent from the showroom for less than ten minutes before returning to instruct her to fetch Bates immediately.

'Were you already aware that Bates and her follower, Carter, had previously been discovered visiting the premises illicitly?' asked Justin.

'Oh, yes. Madame tells me everything – well, most everything,' Parker added, on a note of caution. 'I'd have been pleased to turn that girl off, but for the difficulty that she'd make rouble. She was never a good worker – a lazy slut, if you ask me. And the way she spoke to Madame! Fair shameful, it was!'

'What did you think of the scheme to remove the body?'

She shuddered, her face paling. 'I didn't like it at all, sir. Don't seem right, interfering with the dead, does it? But Madame had the business to think of, and the scandal – but what's to become of us now?'

Her words ended in a wail.

'So let's examine the events of that Monday afternoon in the light of what we've managed to learn from witnesses,' said Justin, rumpling his dark hair in a typical gesture.

'*If* the aforesaid witnesses can be trusted.'

'You sound like a demmed lawyer, Joe. I concede the point academically, but intuition tells me that two of them – Madame and Parker – are being truthful this time. Very well, I know – intuition is for females! Nevertheless, if one considers the Frenchwoman guilty, the question of a reasonable motive arises. *Cui bono*? as our classical tutors would have demanded.'

'Never had none, sir, but I takes y'r meaning. What good would it do her? None that I can see. Brought her naught but trouble.'

'Precisely. And then there's the matter of the method – shooting. I doubt she could have fired the shot, even had she possessed a weapon. So I propose to assume her innocent for the moment, and draw up a timetable of events in an endeavour to examine the opportunities of other possible suspects.'

They had returned to Justin's rooms in Albemarle Street and were at present seated at their ease in the snug bookroom. Justin rose to cross to the mahogany roll top desk, provided himself with pen and paper, and for the next ten minutes or so was busy compiling a list.

At the conclusion of this effort he read the result over with Watts, who agreed that the summary was correct according to their information.

'So what can we deduce from this?' asked Justin.

'Well sir, we've three persons we reckon might have wished deceased out of the way, and they were all in the vicinity of the shop that afternoon. Take Lord Escott, for a start. As the Frenchwoman said, there was that old grudge from the days in Brighton – '

Justin nodded. 'Only consider, Joe, what a revenge to kill your erstwhile rival in the home of the woman who jilted you! Worthy of Greek tragedy, what?'

Watts cast his eyes up to the ceiling, as one making allowance for his former captain's unfortunate classical education.

'And then, of course,' continued Justin, 'there's the more pragmatic motive of the money from their partnership. Wonder how badly he was in need of funds? We must discover that, also the nature of the business they shared.'

'Last of all, sir, he might have got more'n a bit impatient because deceased wasn't making any headway in the match with Miss Jermyn, and decided he'd do better with the uncle out of the way.'

'It's all plausible enough,' declared Justin, with a frown, 'but it may come to nothing. Did he have the opportunity to commit murder?'

They both bent over the timetable again.

'He did,' pronounced Watts. 'Madam saw him at a quarter to three across the road from the shop. It was almost an hour later that she heard what might have been the fatal shot. Ample time to slip in by the door in the side street, shoot Jermyn, and then make good his escape, most like by the basement way.'

'We're assuming, of course, that this was a premeditated, cold blooded murder, and therefore that Escott knew of Jermyn's assignation for that afternoon and meant to seize his chance. The street door was open, providing access for anyone who was aware of that. We know also that Escott was familiar with the premises, having used the private room himself. So far, so simple. But – and it's a big but, Joe – where did he conceal himself while the lovers were together? He couldn't have entered the room without being observed, and there seemed no place of concealment in the main passage, as far as I could see.'

'No, can't say I could,' admitted Watts, ruefully. 'Best go back and go over it all again thoroughly, as we weren't looking special for that when we were there. I s'pose he might have hung about on the stairs leading to the upper storey, but then how would he know when the lady slung her hook, and it was all right for him to go into the room and shoot Jermyn? He couldn't hardly look through that window into the room, on account of it's too high up without standing on a chair or some such. And he daren't hang about outside in the passage for fear he might run across the workpeople.'

'The only possible way for the murderer to lie in wait, as far as I could tell, was to make use of the cloak cupboard in that room. Which would mean, of course, that he – or she – must have been able to get in to the room *before* Jermyn arrived at about ten minutes after two o'clock.'

Watts pursed his lips. 'Seems to rule out Escott, don't it? Unless we can find another hidey hole for him, that is – and a peephole, too,' he added, gloomily.

'Mm, yes. We're at a stand there, for the present. Shall we consider our two other candidates? Pryme, to begin with. His fanatical family pride *may* possibly have driven him over the edge into murder. It's feasible that he could have done it between a quarter past three, when he first called at the salon for Lady St Clare, and just after ten minutes to four, when he returned. Allow five minutes taken up in conversation with Madame at the first call, and there's still a half-hour left. What d'you think, Joe?'

'Plenty of time, guv'nor, as I see it. He'd know Madam would warn the pair at once, and that the lady would fly back to the showroom like a scalded cat, leaving the coast clear for him to confront Jermyn. What's more, *he's* the only one of our suspects we're certain knew about Jermyn being there with her ladyship. Only thing is, would he know his way about behind the showroom?'

'Madame pointed out that any one of her staff might have supplied that information to the murderer. You'll recall, too, that Pryme himself was reported as saying that he could command faithful service. What if you question them again, see if anyone admits to it? There's another matter,' He frowned. 'It may be nothing at all to do with the murder, but I think it would be as well to learn a little more about this follower of Parker – what did she say the fellow's name was?'

Watts consulted his notebook.

'Trimble, sir – William Trimble. She didn't know who employed him, but thought he was in service.'

'We'll see what else she can tell us. To consider the third of our suspects, Blake. We've little to go on here but the report I had of a violent quarrel between that gentleman and Jermyn over Miss Jermyn, a quarrel where they almost came to blows. I don't need to point out to you that a mill between two men in a passion is another case altogether from cold blooded murder, which it becomes increasingly evident that this is. Whoever did it knew where Jermyn would be on that Monday afternoon and laid plans to kill him there, no doubt thinking it a safer location than any other which suggested itself. I don't somehow think that Blake's a strong contender.'

'All the same, with respect, sir, don't do to rule him out,' insisted Watts. 'Love's a powerful emotion, as I'm sure you'll not deny, and this young feller seems to have taken a rare shine to Miss Jermyn. Bit of a hothead, too, by all accounts. Might have thought – as Lord Escott might have done – that he'd stand a better chance with the lady's uncle out of the way. As for opportunity, all we know for sure is that he met Miss Blake outside the shop around four o'clock. Who's to say where he was before that, or what he was doing?'

'True – we must try and find out. Possibly my niece might be entrusted with that task – she's mad as fire to be doing something to help on matters. And if he were to be questioned officially, we'd have to show our hand about the murder having taken place at the salon. We don't want that yet – keep it dark for a bit, if possible.'

CHAPTER XV

Sunlight glinting through a stained glass window cast a blue, ethereal light about the bowed heads of Lady Jermyn and her niece as they stood side by side in their accustomed pew.

It was their first appearance in church since the unfortunate demise of Sir Aubrey Jermyn, and as such aroused a certain amount of politely restrained interest in the other members of the congregation. It was privately agreed among the ladies that Charlotte Jermyn was fortunate in finding that black, often a trying colour for females, did not become her ill; and that the same could not be said of her aunt.

On the opposite side of the aisle the Earl of Pryme grimly shepherded in his son and daughter-in-law, Viscount and Viscountess St Clare, his keen eyes under their bushy brows glancing swiftly about him as he did so. The family did not appear in church very frequently, but Pryme was determined that at present Lady St Clare should be seen abroad on every possible occasion.

Even less frequent were the visits of Lord Escott, who was seated a few pews back from the Jermyns. Anthea Rutherford nudged her mother on seeing him there, opening wide her fine hazel eyes in a caricature of astonishment. Lady Rutherford began to smile, then recollected herself and hastily turned it into a disapproving look.

'Charlotte's bonnet is prodigiously becoming,' whispered Anthea, craftily.

'Indeed it is,' whispered back her mama. 'But you really must try to give your thoughts a more proper direction, my dear.'

Anthea nodded and looked demure. Nevertheless, she managed to catch the eye of a young man of her acquaintance who was her devoted slave, before fixing her attention upon the service which was just beginning.

The sermon was long and tedious to her way of thinking; but at last it was finished, and shortly afterwards the congregation filed slowly out.

Several members gathered about the bereaved ladies either to express for the first time or else to reiterate their condolences. It was noticeable that Lord Escott had joined them as soon as they emerged from the church porch, and remained firmly fixed at their side. Rupert Blake had no intention of allowing that state of affairs to prevail, however. A quick word in his sister's ear and they both moved forward to join the group.

After a short interval of desultory talk, people began to drift away homewards. Lady Jermyn walked with Viscountess Rutherford and Cassandra Quainton in the direction of the carriages; while Charlotte followed closely attended by Escott, Rupert and Mary Blake, with Anthea and her swain in the rear.

'It's a splendid morning, Miss Jermyn,' said Rupert Blake eagerly. 'A pity to be mewed up in a stuffy carriage, don't you think? Why don't you give me – and Mary, of course – the pleasure of walking you home? Now, do say you will!'

'Unfortunately,' put in Escott, with a sneering drawl, 'I have just put the same suggestion to Miss Charlotte, and she assures me that she is too tired for pedestrian exercise.'

Blake favoured him with a hostile glare.

'That don't surprise me!' he snarled.

'Dear me,' said Escott, in steely accents, 'I fear you mean to be insulting, my dear fellow.'

'Damme, I'm not your dear fellow!' exploded Blake.

Escott appeared to consider this. 'No, I believe you are right,' he announced, at last. 'In fact, one can't escape the conviction, Blake, that few people are likely to apply such a term to you.'

At this, Blake's face became suffused with anger, and he clenched his fists at his sides. Mary Blake took his arm, shaking it a little.

'Come, gentlemen, don't let us have any such nonsense on our way home from church! It can scarce be thought appropriate, as I'm sure you'll agree.'

'Pray excuse me a moment,' said Charlotte, hastily detaching herself from the group. 'I particularly wish to speak to Anthea Rutherford.'

She walked quickly over to Anthea, who was still indulging in a gentle flirtation with the moonstruck young man. At sight of Charlotte's somewhat harassed countenance, she speedily dismissed him, taking her friend's arm.

'What's amiss, my love?' she asked. 'You look to be in a sad taking! Has that brute Escott been badgering you? I tried to shake off Brotherton when I saw Escott was clinging to you like a limpet, but there was no discouraging the wretched creature – and, truth to tell, I do quite enjoy flirting with him, as long as I'm not obliged to keep it up for more than ten minutes or so! But tell me what it is, do.'

'Oh, nothing but that Rupert Blake and Escott are at each other's throats, because they both wish to walk me home,' explained Charlotte. 'It's so tiresome, for Rupert is stupid enough to play into Escott's hand, exposing himself in a way which must make Mary feel – as I do – vastly embarrassed! I verily believe, Anthea, that Rupert's ready to do a *mischief* to Escott – oh!' She stopped, clapping a hand to her mouth. 'Perhaps I shouldn't have said that,' she amended. 'But he has such a violent, quick temper, that one wonders – one wonders – '

'I said much the same to Justin, not so long since,' admitted Anthea. 'I felt it necessary to break my promise to you, by the way, not to divulge the fact that Rupert had asked your uncle for permission to address you. I trust you'll forgive me, Lottie, and not set me down as a tattler, for you must realise it's no such thing! Only when it's a matter of murder, ordinary reticences must give way – and Justin posed the direct question to me.'

Charlotte nodded. 'Of course I understand, and think you did right, my love. And it's difficult to refuse to answer Mr Rutherford, when he looks at one in that disarming way of his, is it not?'

Anthea laughed. 'I'm sure you find it so!'

Not so very far away from the sacred edifice in which several members of the *ton* were gathered on that Sunday morning, stood a humbler place of worship. This was a chapel erected almost fifty years previously in the region of Soho Square, and given over to the Nonconformist faith.

The congregation gathered there was somewhat larger than in the fashionable church, and certainly more animated. Hymns were sung with fervour and no one yawned through the sermon.

Miss Parker, seated uncomfortably on a bare wooden bench between a fat, asthmatic female in rusty black and a tailor's apprentice with sharp elbows, heaved a deep sigh from time to time. There was no sign of Mr Trimble in the chapel; perhaps she was fated never to see him again. To add to her misery, her future employment was uncertain. Madame Yvonne, after further questioning at Bow Street, had been released on bail for the time being, chiefly owing to the influence of the Honourable Justin Rutherford.

Justin had represented to Sir Nathaniel Conant, the chief magistrate, that to clap the Frenchwoman into Newgate and close the shop at that stage might not be in the best interests of their investigation. But there was no saying, reflected Miss Parker gloomily, how long this state of affairs would prevail; and where was she to find another good situation in the only trade she understood?

Although she attended regularly at the chapel, she was a woman with few friends, so she walked home alone to her modest lodging in a seedy but respectable side turning off Oxford Street. It was a fine day, so a reluctance to shut herself up indoors made her decide to take a walk along the main thoroughfare.

The pavements were thronged with people strolling along in their Sunday best. She enjoyed the bustle about her, feeling less lonely because of it, and sharing vicariously in their fellowship.

Presently, a face she recognised emerged from among the rest. Its owner made as if to hurry past her, unseeing, but she called out, extending an arm towards him.

'Mr Trimble!'

The man thus addressed paused, started to move on, then changed his mind and came to her side.

'Miss Parker.' He raised his hat punctiliously.

She extended a hand, forcing him to take it.

'I've this moment come from chapel, Mr Trimble,' she said, hesitatingly, for his look was not welcoming. 'You weren't there. I suppose business prevented you?'

He nodded brusquely. 'That's so, ma'am, and I fear I can't stay above a minute or two, now.'

He pulled out his watch and consulted it.

'Yes, I understand,' she said, hurriedly. 'But pray don't go until I've explained how it was I failed to keep our last appointment. I tried hard to get away to meet you in the yard at ten minutes to two, as we agreed, but I couldn't manage it until twenty minutes later. By then, you'd gone. I do trust – that is, I thought perhaps you were vexed, as I'd seen nor heard nothing of you since? I do hope not – I couldn't help it.'

'Yes, yes, I understand.' He fidgeted, obviously anxious to escape. 'Think no more of it.'

'But we'll meet again, won't we?' she asked desperately, putting a hand on his arm. 'Only best not at the shop, because there's been trouble and one o' them Bow Street Runners is hanging about – '

'Bow Street?' he repeated, sharply.

She nodded. 'They came yesterday – the Runner and a gentleman – asking questions of Madame and me. It's on account of that Sir Aubrey Jermyn.'

'The gentleman who was found murdered about a fortnight since near Guy's hospital?'

The urgency had gone out of Mr Trimble's intended departure.

'Yes, him. Only – ' she sank her voice to a whisper – 'he wasn't killed there, but in our shop. And Madame had someone shift him for fear the scandal would harm our business. Somehow they've found out, so now Lord only knows what'll come of it. But you and me can still see each other, can't we?'

'Yes – yes, indeed. But I may be taking another post out of London soon, so I can't quite say – In any case, we mustn't meet at the shop, as you rightly point out. I must go now – an urgent appointment – but I'll seek you out soon at your lodging. Good day, Miss Parker.'

He doffed his hat, and disappeared into the crowd before she could say another word.

'Good of you to see me, Mr Leasowe. I believe Lady Jermyn has prepared you for my visit?'

'Yes, that is so. Please to be seated, Mr Rutherford. I

think you'll find that chair tolerable.'

The lawyer adjusted the spectacles over his nose and indicated a leather armchair near a window looking out on the green of Lincoln's Inn Fields. Sitting down himself behind his desk, he looked expectantly at his visitor.

'You may perhaps wonder at my involvement in Lady Jermyn's affairs,' began Justin.

'No such thing,' replied the other, with a twinkle in his eye. 'Miss Charlotte explained to me how it came about, you see.'

He appraised the gentleman before him with the practised regard of his profession, and decided that here was not only a man to be trusted, but probably one with more than average intelligence. One, too, he concluded whimsically, who would certainly impress a young lady favourably.

'Capital – then I need not enter into tiresome explanations,' Justin continued. 'And as I don't wish to waste more of your time – which I'm sure is valuable – than necessary, I'll come straight to the point. Miss Jermyn told me that her late uncle and Lord Escott were engaged in a business enterprise of some kind, the proceeds of which were to revert to the survivor in the event of the death of either partner.'

Leasowe nodded. 'That is so.'

'You did not deal with the deed, but I collect that you're perfectly satisfied as to its legality?'

'Oh, yes. Lord Escott's man of business, Tysall, of Harbour, Tysall and Storch, dealt with it. I know the firm well – reputable, decidedly.'

'You didn't think it odd that Jermyn didn't consult you at all? In such matters, surely both parties are usually represented by their respective legal advisers?'

'The honest answer to that is yes, Mr Rutherford,' replied Leasowe, with another twinkle. 'If I may be quite frank, I don't think my client wished me to know – er – what he was up to.'

'Ah! Thank you for being frank, sir, and now I'll ask you to be even more so. Miss Jermyn asked you what was the nature of this business and you told her you didn't know.'

'Quite true. I did.'

'But she had the feeling that you did know, though you were reluctant to divulge the information to her. She also asked the same question later of Escott, and he, too, fobbed her off.'

'The deuce she did!' exclaimed the lawyer, jolted momentarily out of his imperturbability. 'That was a trifle – hm! – indiscreet, shall we say?'

'But very natural, as I'm sure you'll agree, sir. Miss Jermyn was also persuaded that you'd have been more ready to supply the information to a male rather than a female.'

Leasowe shook his head ruefully. 'That young lady is altogether too perspicacious – but vastly charming, nevertheless.'

Justin grinned. 'I'd agree on both counts. So now, Mr Leasowe, can I prevail upon you to confide that knowledge to me?'

'I see no reason why not, since my client is deceased. Neither party wished their association in the concern to become public knowledge for reasons which will be obvious. The business is carried on at a house in King Street, and is designated a club – Croker's Club. In actual fact, it is a gambling hell of the most dubious kind, and several young women of easy virtue are employed there as hostesses. It's been raided once by the officers at Bow Street, but that was some years ago, and it's received no attention since. The ownership of the club didn't come to light, and so far still remains secret. Which was exactly as the proprietors desired.'

Justin whistled. 'I can see why you didn't care to explain that to the Jermyn ladies. I must take a look at this club, I think, if I can find someone who's a member. Bit out of my line, gambling hells – healthier at White's or Brooks's if one fancies a hand of cards.'

'My dear sir, you are very right. Although fortunes have been lost and won even in those exclusive establishments.'

'Aye, but it ain't necessary to break open the dice there when one fancies a friendly game of hazard,' said Justin, bluntly.

'True. So if you do go there, Mr Rutherford, at least you know what to expect.'

'I wonder, now,' went on Justin, ruminatively, 'does Escott stand in need of extra funds? I understand that the income from this business venture is considerable.'

'Indeed it is. As for Escott's financial position, it would be indiscreet of me to repeat rumours.'

'But you've heard 'em?' asked Justin, quickly.

The lawyer nodded. 'Reverses on 'change – there may be nothing in it, of course.'

'Thank you. There is one other item of information I'd be grateful if you could see your way to letting me have. Sir George Jermyn, the new baronet – can you tell me anything about him, other than that he's the son of Jermyn's cousin?'

Leasowe cast a shrewd glance at his visitor.

'I can see the way your mind's running, of course. Sir George – an admirable young man, doubtless, though a shade – shall we say stiff – at present. I don't know as yet if he will wish to retain me as his adviser, so perhaps I may consider myself at liberty to – ah – discuss his affairs. To confess truth, I know little of him. His family lived in Tunbridge Wells, but I believe the house was sold on the death of his father in a hunting accident a few years ago. He has spent the past few years roving about, including a stay on the Continent, without any fixed abode. I traced him by an advertisement, and he answered from a locality somewhere in Hertfordshire. I have the letter here, and there's no reason I can see why you may not look at it.'

He rose to reach down a file from one of the shelves and, extracting a letter from it, handed it to his visitor.

Justin read the few lines it contained, then looked up.

'May I keep this for a few days, sir? I undertake to return it safely to you.'

The lawyer hesitated momentarily, then nodded permission.

'I can see no harm in that,' he conceded. 'By the way, perhaps I should inform you that I am completely satisfied as to Sir George's papers of identification. I examined them thoroughly. There is no possibility of fraud.

CHAPTER XVI

It was not usual for Madame Yvonne to close the salon at noon on a Monday, but her two male callers had insisted upon this, and she was in no position to refuse. They had said that she could most probably open her doors again well before two o'clock, and with that she had to be satisfied. Even at her present low ebb of spirits, she could not entirely forget her concern for the business. However, business was slack on a Monday, and it happened to be raining, besides.

Justin and Watts were standing in the passage leading from the street door to the private room, carefully examining their surroundings.

'We're agreed that unless the murderer entered the premises before Jermyn and concealed himself in the cloaks cupboard in yonder room – ' with a nod of his head towards Madame's private apartment – 'he must have had some place of concealment in this passage where he could also look into the room and spy upon its occupants. But where, for God's sake?'

'Dunno, gov'nor, and that's a fact. He could hide on the stairs just round that bend, but he couldn't see into the room from there. The window's at t'other end of the passage. And there's no other hiding place that I can see.'

'Yet it must have been done,' mused Justin. 'Someone knew of this assignation and decided to murder Jermyn here. To accomplish this, he'd need to watch the lovers in their den, and confront Jermyn after the lady had fled, leaving him alone. Only Blake, of all our suspects, might have been able to enter the place *before* Jermyn. The others were seen outside in the street too late for that to be possible. And only Pryme knew when Jermyn would be alone in the room. I wonder now – '

He broke off suddenly, striding down the short passage which led into the salon. Ouside the door of the small storeroom he halted, opened it and entered. Watts followed.

'The first time we looked over the premises, we did no more than glance in here. Now I think we should examine more closely the wall which divides it from the private room.'

In order to do this, they were obliged to move the two large trunks which they had observed on that first occasion. One of these, reflected Justin grimly, had been used to remove Jermyn's body. He opened the lids of both, but no traces of such usage remained; they were scrupulously clean. They had been pushed back almost against the wall, which was shelved from a height of about three feet off the ground as were all the other walls of the room, to accommodate sundry rolls of cloth.

They removed the rolls from the first few rows of shelves, and examined the wall behind in the hope of finding some means of seeing into the room beyond; but to no avail. Justin was about to suggest that they should try the shelves higher up, when another idea came to him.

He stooped and examined the wall immediately underneath the lowest shelf.

After a few moments, he let out an exclamation of triumph.

'Got it! What d'you think of this, Joe?'

The Runner stooped in his turn, and saw a small aperture in the wall about two inches in depth and six inches long, immediately against the underside of the shelf.

'No one would notice this in the ordinary way – who goes about peering under shelves? Yet anyone kneeling down and looking through this aperture has a clear view of the room beyond,' pronounced Justin, suiting the action to the word. 'And now I think of it, there's a bookshelf at this height in the other room, in the same situation.'

'Anyone could take cover behind these trunks, too, sir, at least for a short time,' Watts remarked. 'There'd be some risk of being seen if Madam or that Parker came into the room and stayed looking at the rolls of cloth, or some such, but I think it was a fair enough gamble, what d'ye reckon?'

Justin nodded. 'We'll have a word with them.'

Madame Yvonne and Miss Parker were sitting in the salon, looking even more ill at ease than the elegant chairs justified. Watts crooked his finger unceremoniously, and both women started to their feet.

'Not yet, Miss Parker – it's Madam we're wanting.'

Yvonne followed him into the storeroom, and Watts closed the door behind her, so that their conversation could not be overheard.

'Are you aware,' asked Justin, 'that there's an aperture in the dividing wall between this room and the next through which it's possible to obtain a view of anyone in there?'

She hesitated, then nodded. 'Yes. I had it made when I first took over the shop. I thought it might be as well to keep an eye on things when I was sitting apart in my private room. That wasn't very often, I may say.'

'Does anyone else among your staff know of this?'

She shrugged. 'Who's to say? Obviously, I wouldn't inform them. But if a girl comes in to sweep the floor, or tidy the shelves, she could perhaps discover it.'

'And Miss Parker?'

'I haven't told her.'

'What of those who used the room for assignations – Jermyn and Escott?'

She grimaced. 'Do you suppose, sir, that they'd be content to know they could be spied upon? No, I would not tell them, as you may understand.'

'Cast your mind back to the afternoon of Jermyn's murder, Madame,' said Justin. 'Can you recall if any of you came into this storeroom between, say, a quarter to three, when Lady St Clare arrived, and a quarter past, when you went to warn the pair that the Earl of Pryme had called?'

'I think every moment of that fateful afternoon is etched forever on my memory,' she replied bitterly. 'No, nobody came in here between those times. The last person to enter was myself with a client, Lady Deanesford. That would be earlier, about a quarter past two, and we were in there for, I suppose, some twenty minutes. I know I was at liberty to attend Miss Rutherford to her carriage, and to receive Lady St Clare, who arrived at the same time. But I've already told you of this.'

'Yes. Thank you. Perhaps you would like to ask Miss Parker to step in here?'

Parker came in with scarcely less trepidation than when they had questioned her previously, and for several minutes could not find her voice.

'Come,' said Justin kindly, at last. 'The worst is over now, you know, and there's nothing to be gained by trying to conceal any knowledge you may possess that will assist us in tracking down the murderer. To begin with, ma'am, were you aware that there is a peep hole in the wall here which enables one to see into the next room?'

She began to shake her head, then changed her mind and agreed that she was aware of the fact.

'When did you discover it?' asked Watts.

'A long time since – several years.'

'Your employer don't know that you're aware of it, though,' he said, accusingly.

'No, I didn't mention it to her. I thought she might not want me to know, as she'd not told me of it herself.'

'Have you told anyone else?'

She looked frightened again, and shook her head.

'What, no one?' persisted Watts. 'Come along, now, we want the truth, mind. Ye may have to come before the magistrate if ye don't deal with us fair and square.'

'Oh, no! No, I will tell you what you want to know, only I've done no wrong – I meant no harm – '

'You told your friend Mr Trimble, did you not?' asked Justin quietly.

She started violently. 'How – how did you know – who told you?' she stammered.

'Don't be afraid, Miss Parker. Tell us more about your friendship with Mr Trimble. We know that he was to meet you here on the day that Jermyn was murdered. Did he come here on any previous occasions?'

She nodded. 'Yes – once or twice he'd called in at the same time for us to arrange meetings. He only stayed a few minutes, though, most times. But once – ' She stopped, a flush creeping into her cheeks.

'Yes?' said Justin, encouragingly.

'He said he wanted to see where I worked – so's he could picture me going about my duties – and Madame chanced to be absent for an hour or so that day, so I was the only one in the salon. I wouldn't have shown him round, only – only – there's no one to care anything about me now Mother's gone, and he did seem to – ' She broke off and covered her face with her hands.

Justin felt an irresistible urge at that moment in the toe of his boot, and wished the mysterious Mr Trimble had been at hand to offer relief to the angry impulse.

They allowed her a few moments to recover, studiously contemplating the wallpaper meanwhile.

'So you showed him everything – the secret entrance to this room and the peephole?' Justin asked presently in a gentle tone.

She gulped and nodded. 'I know I shouldn't have done, but you see – '

'Yes, we do see, and understand. How long since did this occur, ma'am?'

She looked up at him gratefully, thinking what a kind gentleman he was, calling her "ma'am", too, as though she'd been gentry. It was not true, what they said, that the *ton* cared nothing for the feelings of those in a lower social order. Almost she forgot for the moment her suspicion that Mr Trimble had been using her in some obscure way. She smiled at Justin, and he smiled back, his dark eyes full of compassion.

'It must be a month since, sir. Madame had gone to Grafton House to order some new materials. I mind it was on a Monday, for that's our slack day for business.'

Justin made a mental note that this would be a fortnight before the murder took place.

'Can you give us a description of this 'ere Trimble?' demanded Watts, suddenly, producing his notebook.

'A description?' she faltered.

'Yes, what did he look like?' Watts interpreted.

She pondered for a moment. 'I can't rightly say. He's most gentlemanlike, neatly dressed and speaks proper. Not tall, nor yet short, middling height, I'd say. Middling size altogether, for he's not thin, nor yet fat – '

'Is he dark or fair haired? How old is he?'

'Not rightly dark, more middling brown, I'd say,' she answered, frowning in an effort to do her best to answer correctly. 'As to age, middle years, about like you, Mr

Watts, though perhaps a few years older.'

Watts sighed in exasperation. 'A middling sort of cove altogether, it seems. Ah well, I dare say you're doin' yer best. And ye haven't seen this cully since he made that appointment ye couldn't keep, for the day of the murder?'

She started. 'Oh, no! I saw him yesterday, after I'd been to chapel.'

Justin and Watts exchanged glances.

'Where was this, ma'am? Perhaps you'll be good enough to tell us about it.'

'Certainly I'll do my best, but it was all so quick, you see. I was walking along Oxford Street and suddenly I saw him in the crowd. He was in a hurry, so couldn't stay to say much. I told him how it was I failed to meet him as we'd arranged on that day. He said it didn't matter, and was for hurrying off, but I asked him – ' she flushed a little – 'when we'd meet again, and said it would be best not at the shop, because of the murder, and Bow Street Runners nosing around, and all. He seemed struck by that, so I explained about the murder – '

'Had he heard of that? asked Justin, sharply.

She nodded. 'Yes, but he thought like everyone else that the – body – had been found near Guy's hospital. So I told him the truth of it. Then he said we should meet again, but he'd be taking a post outside London, so he couldn't promise when. Then he had to hurry off,' she added, disconsolately.

'I see. Well, ma'am, should you encounter Mr Trimble again, we'd be obliged if you'd let us know at once.'

She paled. 'You don't think – he's not – oh, no, *he* couldn't have had aught to do with it!'

'That's as may be,' said Watts, grimly. 'But anyone hangin' about this shop on that particular day interests us, miss.'

'But he wasn't!' she protested, quickly. 'Leastways, he

wasn't there when I went down to the yard.'

'Not to say as he hadn't been and gone, is it? Ye said yourself he only stayed a few minutes as a rule.'

'What harm could he do in a few minutes, then?' she demanded, stung into truculence in defence of her follower.

'We'll be the judge o'that,' answered Watts promptly. 'Just ye do as we asks, else ye'll be in trouble, too, and so I warn ye.'

She said no more, and Justin dismissed her politely.

'So what d'ye reckon now, sir?' asked Watts, when they were alone. 'Seems a good many folk could have known of this spy hole, and passed the information on to interested parties.'

'Yes, indeed. The trouble with this case, Joe, is that we've only suspicion to go on, and not a vestige of proof so far. According to our timetable, the murder was most likely committed at twenty minutes to four, when Madame heard what must have been a shot. The murderer would clear out almost at once, by way of the backstairs and the mews. It's possible that someone may have seen him leaving – indeed, it's our only chance of proof. Question the rest of the staff again, Joe, see if they recall anything. You'll do better with them than I shall. Meanwhile, I've a few other ploys to occupy me.'

Watts nodded. 'I can hazard a guess – the baronet and the gambling hell, eh? What do'ye reckon to this man Trimble, sir?'

'A good question, Joe. I do have a notion as to where he fits into the puzzle, and it's one of the matters for my attention. I think, too, he may not be far to seek. But we shall see.'

CHAPTER XVII

The landlord at the Cricketers' Inn, Croxfield, looked somewhat overwhelmed at having entrusted to his care what he termed a spanking turn-out and a pair of prime bits of blood; but he rallied manfully when the driver of this handsome equipage explained that it would be only for a short time. After all, the Cricketers was no posting inn.

'I've a good man in the stable to tend the cattle, y'r honour,' he promised. ' 'Bain't much old Ned don't know about the Quality's horses – used to be head groom up to the Manor, until Sir Peter died, and the old place was let to come-who-may. Ye'll be visitin' up there, no doubt? A Mr Waterman's the tenant at present – been there close on a year – dare say he's a friend o' yourn?'

'Regret I haven't that pleasure. However, I intend to make his acquaintance this afternoon, should he be at home,' returned the pleasant young man. 'Oblige me with a tankard of your home brewed, landlord, for I've a powerful thirst.'

'Thirsty weather, y'r honour,' agreed mine host, leading the way through the cobbled yard into the best parlour the small establishment could boast. 'Sit ye down, sir, and I'll bring it at once.'

Justin Rutherford obeyed, looking appreciatively about him. There were few places, he reflected, more truly comfortable than the average English inn parlour. Gleaming oak settles and tables, bright chintz covers and a low-ceilinged, timbered room with a wide, open fireplace provided a setting very much to his taste. So, too, was the home brewed ale when it arrived. He tossed it down, then took his way out of the inn, having enquired of the landlord the way to the Manor.

He sauntered across the wide village green, where several women were gathered about the well drawing water and indulging in a good gossip. They stared at him in friendly curiosity, but turned away embarrassed as he smiled at them. A stony track led past a row of cottages to the Manor.

He paused at the wrought iron gates, surveying the building appreciatively. It was a Tudor house, with tall, twisted chimneys and mullioned windows. He grimaced at the superimposed modern pillared portico. Who could possibly commit such an act of vandalism? But then not everyone had his own feeling for historic buildings.

A footman received his card without interest, and invited him to step inside. In a few moments, he was shown into an oak panelled room with an intricately decorated plaster ceiling and diamond paned windows looking out on to a velvety lawn bounded by topiary work.

The man who came forward to greet him was of much the same age as himself, but of a more portly build, with a round, good natured countenance.

'Mr – Rutherford,' he said, glancing at the card.

Justin gave a short bow. 'Afraid we're not acquainted, sir. Apologise for disturbing you.'

The other returned the bow. 'Not at all. Y'r servant, sir – my name's Waterman. Pray sit down. Can I offer you anything?'

'No, thank you. I've just sampled the home brewed at the Cricketers, and very good it is. But I won't waste your time, Mr Waterman. I believe there is a gentleman staying here – perhaps a connection of yours? – named Jermyn, George Jermyn?'

The good humour faded from Mr Waterman's face and he scowled.

'He was staying here,' he replied, shortly. 'He's been gone almost a week. Friend of yours, sir?'

'No. I merely wished to see him on a matter of business,' said Justin, glibly.

Waterman gave a short laugh. 'So did all the others.'

'I beg your pardon?'

'You're chasing him for debts, I'll be bound. Since he left here, it's been nothing but Jermyn's creditors knocking on my door, day after day. I deny myself to the most obvious duns – damme, what's a man to do? But your card, the Honourable Justin Rutherford – might have been for me.'

'My dear sir, it sounds as though you've been having a thin time of it. Is Sir George Jermyn a family connection, since he was staying in your house?'

'Devil a bit of it! Matter of fact, I met him while I was on a visit to Paris earlier in the year. He was plain Mister then – hadn't come into the baronetcy. Told me of that before he left. You know how it is in a foreign country, I dare say – Englishmen get together in the clubs and cafés, ready to accept each other at face value. He seemed able to sport the ready over there, all right and tight. Can't say he was just in my style, besides being a good bit younger, but when I left for home I said in parting, as one does, y'know, to look me up when he returned. Never thought he would, of course.'

Justin nodded sympathetically.

'When did he arrive at your home, Mr Waterman, and did he come straight here from France?'

'Indeed he did. Landed on my doorstep with all his luggage, asked if I could put him up for a night or two. That was nigh on a month since. What was I to do? Look deuced shabby to hint him away, but I scarce knew the man.'

'When he quitted the Manor, did he leave a direction with you where you might communicate with him or forward him any correspondence?'

'No such thing. Hasn't had the courtesy so far to send me the conventional letter of thanks for putting him up. Not that I'm one to stand on points, mind you, but, damme, any gentleman's going to observe the courtesies, don't you think?'

'I do indeed. Tell me, sir, did Sir George pass all his time here with you at the Manor and in the immediate neighbourhood? Or did he perchance go up to Town on occasion?'

'Oh, yes, for the odd day, y'know, but not to stay overnight. He told me he had no acquaintance in London – seems he'd never met his cousin Jermyn – and knowing what I do now, I'll wager he'd not lodge anywhere if it meant sporting his blunt for it!'

'I wonder if you can recall whether he paid one of these visits precisely a fortnight ago, on a Monday?'

Mr Waterman's shaggy eyebrows shot up. 'Something's in the wind, eh? What's he been up to?'

'Perhaps nothing at all. But I would be vastly obliged to you if you could answer my question.'

The other man considered for a moment, then nodded.

'Yes, he did. I recall that he'd also been up to Town on the previous Friday, so when he went off on the Monday, so soon afterwards, I began to hope that he might be moving on to lodge there permanently. No such luck, though, for he remained fixed here until Thursday of last week, when thank God he left for good. Told me he'd come into a title and estate on account of his cousin's death. And a good riddance, say I.'

Justin looked in at White's that evening, and found several friends and acquaintances there. He managed to avoid being drawn into a game of cards by saying that he was unable to stay long; and after chatting to one and another in a desultory fashion, was able to achieve the real purpose of his visit, which was to talk with some of the late Sir Aubrey's particular friends. He came upon the Honourable Nigel Ambrose seated alone, glancing through a copy of a magazine while he awaited some crony late in arriving for an engagement.

Justin's acquaintance with Mr Ambrose was naturally slight, since they were of different generations, but he made the approach with his usual address. A few civil but commonplace remarks led on to the subject of Jermyn's murder.

'Shocking business,' agreed Mr Ambrose. 'And dooced puzzlin', into the bargain. Mean to say, don't seem to be an ordinary affair of footpads – not that there's anything ordinary about having one's brains beaten out by thugs, at any time! But there's more to this than meets the eye, if you ask me. Someone had it in for poor old Aubrey, not a doubt of it. Wonder if they'll ever lay the feller that did it by the heels? Not that one would want it if he chanced to be – well, y'know – one of us.'

Justin nodded. 'Quite,' he replied. 'Have you chanced to meet the new baronet, Sir George Jermyn, as yet?'

'Matter of fact, I have. Feller called in at the Club to see Aubrey a few days before his death. Seems this cousin had written to say he was staying in Hertfordshire and would like to meet his relative, so Aubrey wrote back in that casual way of his to say drop in at the Club any time he chanced to be in Town. Aubrey hoped he wouldn't, of course – never wondrous great on relatives, Aubrey, and he'd never met this feller, after all. But he turned up on this particular day – a Friday, I think it was – so of course Aubrey had to introduce him to a few of us. Soon got rid of him, though – bit of a starched up young feller, we thought.'

'Can't say – I've not met him myself. Have you seen him about Town at all since?'

Nigel Ambrose shook his head, then flung up his hand in a gesture to recall the denial.

'Wait a moment, though – saw him on the Monday Aubrey disappeared, yes, of course I did! He came here again, but went off when he was told his cousin wasn't in the Club. Thought I saw him later on, too, when I was strollin' down Bond Street with Davenport – but may have been mistaken – only caught a glimpse of the feller in a crowd.'

'What time would that be?' asked Justin, as carelessly as he was able.

Fortunately, Mr Ambrose's intellect was not of the highest order, or he might have found some purpose in these questions. He gave the matter his consideration.

'Say around three o'clock,' he pronounced at last. 'See a good many people strollin' down Bond Street at that time of day – saw Escott, come to think of it, and Pryme, not to speak of females shoppin' – the lovely St Clare female for one. A diamond of the first water, she is, m'boy!'

Justin agreed, and deftly turned the conversation to Escott.

'Can't stand the feller,' said Nigel Ambrose. 'Always tryin' to quiz one. Never could understand why he and Aubrey were so thick together, for I don't think they liked each other above half.'

'Perhaps it was a business friendship,' suggested Justin,

as one who does not really believe it.

'Business? Good God, Aubrey had no head for business! Besides, all one hears lately of Escott, he's had some deep doings in the stock market, so who'd be such a gudgeon as to join him, I ask you?'

'Has he, indeed? Not in the River Tick, is he?'

'Good God, no, just a trifle under the hatches. Leave investments to your broker, say I. Still, he's sure to come about, a well breeched feller like him.'

'Talking of gambling,' said Justin, idly, 'do you know anything about a hell named Croker's, situated in King Street, so I'm told?'

'Get your fingers burnt there, m'boy, so don't risk it,' advised Mr Ambrose. 'I went once with Cardice, who's a member, and although I was more than a bit on the go at the time, I could tell I'd got in among the sharks. No, do your gaming in White's and Brooks's, my dear feller, that's my tip.'

The Earl of Pryme's butler looked down his long nose at the respectable but undistinguished man standing on the doorstep.

'You're quite sure his lordship made an appointment with you?' he demanded loftily, slightly accenting the last word.

The man appeared undeterred by this cold reception.

'Perfectly sure. And if you'll be good enough to inform his lordship that Mr Preston awaits his pleasure, you will find that I'm expected.'

'You'd best step inside,' returned the butler grudgingly. 'Wait here.'

He trod his dignified way across the chequered hall towards a passage leading to the Earl of Pryme's library. Half way along, he encountered Ruth, Lady St Clare's personal maid.

'Who is it?' she asked, *sotto voce*.

'Preston, valet to the late Sir Aubrey Jermyn. You'll know the man slightly, as I do myself. Says he has an appointment with his lordship – seems odd to me.'

'It wouldn't be the first time,' she confided, 'but as a rule he don't come to the house.'

The butler stared. 'Not much misses you, Ruth, and that's a fact. What's it all about, eh?'

She shook her head. 'Ah, that'd be telling. Hadn't you best be on your way to announce the caller, Mr Ridge?'

He gave her an unfriendly look before continuing down the passage. She hesitated for a moment, then slipped into an anteroom adjoining the library.

'What the devil d'ye mean by coming here?' the Earl greeted his visitor truculently. 'I said I'd see you in the stables – not that I can see any occasion now for meeting at all.'

'Perhaps not for you, my lord,' replied Preston, standing his ground. 'There is for me, however.'

'What d'ye mean?' roared the Earl

He was unusued to defiance from anyone, servant or family.

'It's necessary for me to seek another situation now, as your lordship will realise.'

'So? I dare say this new man – whatsisname? – Sir George Jermyn – will take you on. If not, there's always the employment agencies. Either way, it ain't no concern of mine, so if that's all you came to say, you can clear off.'

'Ah, but isn't it any concern of yours, my lord?' asked Preston, silkily. 'Are you certain of that?'

'What in thunder d'ye mean?'

Pryme's face was suffused with red, and his voice rose in a way that would have terrified any of his own domestic staff, as he started from his chair.

'Consider it for a moment,' suggested Preston, maintaining his cool composure. 'I have been of invaluable service to you, have I not? It may be that there are those who would be interested to learn of our connection, my lord.'

He fell back a pace as the Earl raised a threatening arm, looking as though he was about to go off in a fit of apoplexy.

'Don't harm me!' Preston warned, quickly. 'There are witnesses, remember!'

'You – you! Hell and the devil, I'd wring your neck but for soiling my hands!' exploded Pryme.

For a few moments he could say no more, while he struggled visibly for mastery of his rage. Presently it subsided a little, and he sat down again.

'So you mean to blackmail me, do you, you cur – you unspeakable villain! Well, speak up, then! What d'ye want? What's your price?'

Preston seemed to be master of the situation once again.

'Harsh words, my lord. Nothing so crude as blackmail, I assure you. It is simply that I feel I'd like a change from the position of gentleman's gentleman. I thought perhaps a modest tavern in the country – say Surrey, or Kent – where a man could be at one with Nature, so to speak – '

'Bah! Don't try to gammon me with your high flown flummery! What's your price?'

Preston named a figure, and Pryme's eyebrows shot up.

'Good God! Modest tavern, did you say? Posting inn of the first flight, more like! I'll not pay!'

'That would be a pity, my lord. Only consider how certain quarters – Bow Street, for instance – might be interested in what I could tell them.'

Pryme was visited by another, even more violent, spasm of rage. Wordlessly, he dragged open a drawer in his bureau, removed a cash box from it which he unlocked with shaking fingers, and tossed a wad of banknotes on to the table beside Preston.

'Take it, damn you to hell! It's over the odds, so you needn't trouble to count it! And now get out – but mark this, my man – there'll be no more payments to this account! If you come round a second time on this errand, you know what to expect, don't you? And ye'll get it, mark my words!'

Justin went straight from the Club to Lady Quainton's soirée, which he had promised as a special favour to attend if only for an hour or so. She was delighted to see him, although he was late in arriving; and she indicated that she had something of importance to communicate as soon as she could break free from her duties as hostess.

He looked about a little and soon saw Anthea, looking a vision in pink silk and gauze with a silver thread in the material, her dark hair bound up in a tapering cone with pink and silver ribbons. As usual, she was surrounded by young gentlemen and sharing her favours equally among them, much to their chagrin. He grinned wickedly as he watched them jostling for position, though in the politest way.

Presently he joined the group. Taking her hand, which she extended towards him, he kissed it in an extravagant manner. She dimpled, looking about her at all the envious faces with evident enjoyment.

'An uncle's privilege,' he murmured to them.

'Pray exercise it elsewhere, Rutherford,' protested Philip Randles, who was known to Justin. 'I protest it's more than flesh and blood can bear to watch!'

'What nonsense you do talk,' sparkled Anthea, at her element in this flowery kind of scene. 'But you must permit me to be private with my Uncle Justin for a while, if you please, for there's something I wish to tell him.'

Reluctantly, they all withdrew, and Justin seated himself beside her.

'D'you really care for that kind of flummery?' he asked, scornfully.

'Oh, yes, I find it famous fun – besides, it's all the crack for gentlemen to pay extravagant compliments to ladies. Why, you joined in it yourself, did you not?' she accused.

He shrugged. 'It seemed to be the order of the day, and I couldn't let you down, now, could I? Were you bamming 'em when you said you'd something to tell me, or did you mean it?'

'I meant it, but, oh, Justin, I think you'll be disappointed in what I've found out this time! I've been talking to Mary and Rupert Blake earlier, as you asked me, and he couldn't have had anything to do with the murder, after all. Was ever anything so provoking?'

He laughed. 'I don't suppose he'd agree with you. But what was the reason?'

'He was with two other gentlemen from about one o'clock until just before he and Mary encountered each other outside the salon. It seems they ate a nuncheon together at the Pulteney hotel, strolled a while in Green Park, then went their separate ways about four o'clock. One of them, Mr Clarendon, actually corroborated this, so I'm certain it must be true, without troubling to ask the other.'

Justin nodded. 'Yes, I know Clarendon slightly, and of course he wouldn't lie – no reason why he should. Well, I may say that Blake was never a strong candidate in my view. Kind of chap who might start a mill with another fellow over a quarrel – though hardly with Jermyn, I think, seeing that he was so much older – but not at all likely, I'd say, to commit cold blooded murder. And this was, Anthea, make no mistake.'

She shivered.

'I'm relieved that it doesn't put out your theories, at all events. I did find out one or two other things from Mary, though I don't know whether you'll think them important.'

'Suppose you attempt to discover that?'

She screwed up her face at him.

'Monster! Well, firstly, she agrees with the times Madame Yvonne gave for Pryme's arrival at the salon and Stella St Clare's appearance soon afterwards. Also for his final call, when he departed with Stella about five minutes to four. That was just before Mary herself left, you know. She is always vastly meticulous about details, Justin, I assure you, so I think we can accept what she says.'

'I'm prepared to do so. And secondly?'

'How you do take one up! Well, secondly, she told me that when she was driving along Bond Street towards the salon about three o'clock, she saw Pryme leaning out of his carriage and talking to – whom do you suppose? – none other than Jermyn's valet Preston, who was standing on the pavement. Of course, she's seen him often at the Jermyns', as she and Rupert were there frequently until the murder. Yes, and another odd thing – my maid Martha was strolling about while I was in the salon that fateful day, and she mentioned to me this morning that she'd seen the valet actually *enter* the side door of Madame's premises. It must have been about half past two, for I left there at a quarter to three, as I've told you already. What on earth can he have been doing? Jermyn wouldn't have taken him there, that's certain!'

'I believe he was what my friend Joe Watts would describe as up to no good,' replied Justin, grimly. 'Was this the extent of your friend's revelations? I trust you didn't confide to her the fact that the murder took place at Madame's shop?'

'Of course not! But here comes Aunt Cassie, looking very purposeful.'

It was evident that Lady Quainton was big with news. She wasted no time in preamble, but told Justin at once that her maid Jane had brought her a full account of a conversation overheard by Jane's friend Ruth between the Earl of Pryme and Preston, Jermyn's valet. She repeated the whole.

Justin and Anthea listened intently. At the conclusion, Anthea stared round-eyed at her relative.

'What do you suppose it means, Justin? If the valet is blackmailing Pryme, it can only be – '

Justin glanced swiftly about him, but for the moment there was no one within earshot.

'Best not to discuss it here. I've been coming round to the notion that Preston may have something more to contribute to this investigation than he revealed when I first questioned him. I'll go into it tomorrow. Meanwhile, your ardent admirers are casting languishing glances in this direction. Go and put them out of their misery.'

She looked around, her dark eyes dancing.

'Yes, and talking of languishing glances, Hetty Benedict is obviously wishing that I would take you over to introduce you.'

'Which one is she?' he asked cautiously. 'Not, I trust, the scrawny female with the warts?'

'No such thing – she's that prodigiously attractive girl in the blue silk, over yonder.'

He looked in that direction and leapt to his feet.

'I go a willing sacrifice, my dear. Lead on.'

'Oh, for shame! Poor Charlotte!'

CHAPTER XVIII

Joseph Watts wrinkled his nose as he stepped into one of the sleazy alleys around Covent Garden. The place smelt of cats, or was it something worse, he wondered? The tumbledown houses crowded close together, shutting out the daylight even though it was early in the morning and a fine day. A few dirty, apathetic children loitered about, and a costermonger was setting out with his barrow from one of the houses, otherwise there were few signs of activity. No busy housewives here, shaking the dust from their mats outside as they exchanged a few words of gossip.

The coster gave Watts a wary look as he carefully edged past him with the barrow. This was a fairly respectable neighbourhood compared to the grim rookeries of St Giles or the Ratcliffe Highway, but its inhabitants knew a Bow Street man when they saw him even though the Runners wore no distinguishing uniform.

Watts pushed open the battered door of one of the houses and climbed a short flight of stairs with well worn treads before knocking on the second door along the dim passage.

After a few moments' waiting, the door opened reluctantly an inch or so, and a face peered apprehensively round. It was a young, pretty face, but bore the marks of poverty and deprivation.

'Oh, so it's you, is it? I thought as 'ow ye'd slung yer 'ook fer good an' all.'

'I've a question or two to ask ye yet, my wench, so ye'd best let me come inside,' returned Watts.

Sally Bates shrugged, but stood aside to let him enter, The room was reasonably clean, with no floor covering, a bed in one corner, a table and two kitchen chairs in the centre, and a small fire burning in the grate, with a kettle on the hob. About the walls were disposed a few cooking utensils, and an open shelved cupboard held a scanty stock of tableware.

'Ma's out,' said Sally morosely, 'but she'll be back afore long. What d'ye want o' me? Ye've done me enough 'arm, I reckon.'

'Naught to what I could do, unless ye've the sense to go on bein' King's Evidence,' threatened Watts.

'I've telt ye all I know – leave me be!'

'Cast yer mind back to the day of the murder, wench. When ye was sitting in the basement workroom that afternoon, did ye notice anyone – anyone at all – go past on the way to the yard?'

She screwed up her face in an effort of recall.

'Can't 'ardly see yer work down there, it's that dim. As for peerin' out into the passage – '

'But ye'd hear footsteps going along it.'

She nodded. 'Aye, and I did. Miss Parker's, for one – we can tell 'ers from t'others. She went out one time, come back soon arterwards.'

'Would that be about ten past two?'

'Don't expect me to know the time, do yer? Madame don't keep a clock down there – we might want ter watch it, ha, ha.'

This was said mirthlessly. Watts abandoned that tack, going on to another.

'Reckon ye'd go out into the yard now and then, same as

all the other wenches. Did you happen to see a man hanging about there any time during the last few months, and particularly on the day of the murder?'

'Don't mean them two sapskulls workin' in the stable, do yer? No, I knows who yer mean – Parker's follower.' She threw back her head and laughed. 'Pore ol' Parker – who'd ever think she'd get 'erself a man? Just shows, never give up 'ope, as Ma often says.'

Watts pressed her for a description of Mr Trimble, but he gained no more information than Parker herself had provided.

'Didn't get me ogles on 'im more'n twice or thrice,' she excused herself. 'But 'e weren't no chub, mind.'

'Not a labourer,' translated Watts. 'Would ye say he was gentry, then?'

She looked puzzled, 'Dunno. Tell yer what, though, I catched a sight on another gent that day, just nippin' through the yard gate as I come out o' the privy. Only saw the back on 'im for a minute, but no mistakin' the cut o' Quality clothes, not in this trade.'

Watts was on the alert at once. 'What time was that?'

'Allus on about time,' she mocked. 'Telt ye I never knows down there. Arf a mo', though, mebbe I can 'elp a bit. It weren't much more'n 'arf an hour, I'd reckon, arterwards, that Madame sends for me upstairs. That's by me own reckonin', on account of 'ow much work I'd done on that danged flounce for milady Deanesford's gown. 'Ad to leave it then, o'course.'

'That would be when your employer had found the body and wanted you to fetch Carter to dispose of it?'

She nodded.

'Ye say ye only saw the back of this man. Can you describe him at all? How old was he? Tall or short, fat or thin? What was he wearing?'

She snorted. 'Ask a mort o'questions, don't yer? He was

gone in a flash through the gate as I comed out o' the privy, so I didn't rightly see 'im at all. He wasn't young, I reckon, an' not tall nor short – not like a dwarf, any road. I noticed 'is clothes, 'cos ye do in the trade. Quality, they was – grey trousis an' a blue coat, shiny boots like the toffs wear, an' a tall 'at.'

Watts jotted a few notes down in his book.

'And you went straight back into the basement room afterwards?'

'Yus. Don't pay us ter 'ang about, or we'd 'ave ol' Parker arter us.'

'Did anyone else come downstairs after that, until Parker summoned you upstairs? Think hard, now.'

She screwed up her face again.

'Aye, so there was, now I think on 't. I'd scarce sat at me bench when I 'eard someone going' along the passage to the yard. In a 'urry, too.' she laughed. 'I telt the others 'e was taken short.'

'You say "he", I notice,' Watts interposed sharply. 'You thought it was a man, then?'

She frowned. 'Reckon I must've done – p'raps thought it was one o' them clodpoles from the mews. We knew it wasn't ol' Parker's footsteps, so we didn't trouble ourselves. For a minute, I thought she was arter me fer goin' outside – can't even do that, ye knows. Eh, mister, what's to become o' me now? Me man's in Newgate, an' I'm kep' away from the shop. When can I go back?'

Watts shook his head. 'Likely we'll need ye as a witness before long, my wench, so just you bide here. As for going back, if ye take my tip, ye'll start looking for another job.'

After thankfully shaking off the dust of this uninviting quarter, he walked through to the Strand and took a hackney to Albemarle Street.

He was confident of finding Mr Rutherford at home at

this early hour of the morning. In fact, Justin had only just finished breakfast.

'Ah, glad you looked in, Joe,' he greeted the Runner. 'I've news to impart.'

'Me, too, sir. I've interviewed Madam's workpeople again, as you asked. But mebbe you'd prefer to tell me your news first?'

'It will keep for a bit longer. Let's hear your report.'

'Well, sir, to start at the useless end, there was nothing fresh to be learnt from the two men who work outside, nor three of the wenches in the basement. The men weren't there that afternoon at all, and the seamstresses said the same as they'd said when I questioned them before – they saw nor heard naught. The one who assists Parker in the shop, though – Baines, she's called – she admitted that she showed Miss Rutherford into that cubby hole in mistake for another lady, her not being used to working in the salon, and Parker not being there to keep an eye on her. It don't make any difference to the evidence as far as the murder's concerned, but it clears up that little puzzle. Always satisfactory to get things straight, don't you think, sir?'

'I do indeed, but I can't help hoping that the rest of your report will be more fruitful. From the look in your hawk-like eye, Joe, I'd say it will be.'

Watts grinned. 'Straight to the mark, guv'nor! The wench Bates – a comely little piece, by the way – told me something of real interest.'

He repeated the conversation, with occasional references to his notebook for confirmation.

Justin whistled. 'Mm, that *is* interesting, especially when taken in conjunction with what I learned yesterday evening from Lady Quainton. Here's the gist of it.'

Watts listened attentively.

'Begins to look as if this valet, Preston, did the murder,' he said at the end of the recital.

Then he shook his head, echoing Justin's quick negative.

'No,' he corrected himself. 'Not as he was seen talking to Lord Pryme in the street at three o'clock. Miss Rutherford's maid saw him go in at the side door at twenty-five minutes to three, but he was outside again before the murder, which we've fixed at twenty minutes to four. Won't do, will it?'

'He could have gone back inside again and waited his chance to commit the murder,' said Justin, in the tone of one who postulates a theory. 'But somehow I don't think he's our man. I've a pretty sound notion of where he fits into this puzzle, and I propose that we make our way to Lady Jermyn's and interview him without delay. Interesting, Joe, the girl Bates seeing that individual slip out of the yard gate at what must have been soon after the murder was committed. It's perhaps the most important piece of evidence we have so far.'

'Yes, in a case where hard evidence is remarkably thin,' agreed Watts, lugubriously. 'Never mind, perhaps this cully Preston will give us a bit more to go on.'

'If you could spare me a few moments, my lady,' began Preston, diffidently.

Lady Jermyn looked up from the tambour frame which was set before her, fastened the needle to the canvas, and pushed the work aside.

'Certainly,' she said, affably. 'There's nothing troubling you, I trust, Preston?'

'Only the matter of my future, my lady. Of course, I have no purpose here since – the regrettable decease of my master. I've been considering what best to do – '

'Oh, but of course you have!' exclaimed Lady Jermyn,

sympathetically. 'I dare say you will wish to take another post – but if you do not, and would welcome retirement, then of course I'll speak to Mr Leasowe about a suitable financial arrangement for you.'

'You are very good, my lady.' Preston gave a little bow. 'I must say that I have been considering retirement. After serving a gentleman of fashion who was one of His Royal Highness's select circle, it would be difficult to feel any satisfaction in what could only be an inferior situation. I have therefore decided that, should you be so very good as to make some provision for me, I might find a little place in the country where I could be tolerably content.'

'Yes, yes, of course. I will speak to Mr Leasowe immediately. We shall be very sorry to lose you, of course, for you've always been an invaluable valet, as my husband often remarked. But as things are – '

'Unless,' put in Charlotte, who had been reading but had put the book aside when Preston entered the room, 'our kinsman, the new baronet, might need a valet? That would be a comparable situation for you, although Sir George has no connection with Royalty, so far. Still, one never knows.'

'You are very good, Miss Jermyn, but I consider myself perhaps a little too old to learn the ways of a young gentleman such as Sir George. I shall be happy to accept Lady Jermyn's most kind offer to make arrangements for my future. I thought perhaps, my lady, you would not object if I were to quit your service immediately?'

Lady Jermyn looked surprised.

'Oh, no, naturally I should have no objection. But you'll wish first to confer with my man of business, I suppose? I'll send a message to him today, but he may not be at liberty to wait on me for a few days. However, there's no reason for you to hurry away – you're welcome to keep your rooms for as long as you wish.'

'You are very good, my lady, but I think it will be best if I make a move as soon as I have seen Mr Leasowe. I need scarce tell you, ma'am, that I cannot escape a lowering sensation of melancholy since – however, I'll not refine too much upon that. I'm sure you'll understand.'

She assured him that indeed she did, and that it reflected very much to his credit. He bowed, and quitted the room as silently as he had come.

'You see how easy it is to misjudge people, my love,' remarked Lady Jermyn, when he had gone. 'I never realised that Preston had so much genuine regard for poor Aubrey – I always credited him with being rather a – '

She paused, at a loss for a suitable word.

'Cold fish?' suggested Charlotte. 'I believe he is, and am wondering precisely what lies behind his haste to shake our dust from his feet. I wouldn't be a bit surprised if he hasn't already procured himself an advantageous situation, and means to take the pension you've offered him in addition.'

'Lottie! How can such a sweet, loving girl as you are give way to such – such cynical notions! I declare I don't know how it comes about!'

'Heredity, dearest Aunt – but not from your side. It does not do to be too naive, as one may easily discover to one's cost.'

Lady Jermyn was about to carry her protest further when she was interrupted by the footman, who requested permission to admit Mr Rutherford.

Delight spread at once over Charlotte's face, and Lady Jermyn herself seemed pleased. Justin was ushered into the room at once. After greeting them and asking how they both did, he expressed a wish to be allowed to interview Preston once more.

'He has but this minute been with us, Mr Rutherford,' said Lady Jermyn. 'He was telling us that he felt there was no longer any purpose for him in the household, and the time had come for him to move on.'

'To another post?'

'No, to retirement. I've undertaken to provide him with a pension, of course, in view of his long and faithful service.'

Justin raised his brows. 'I can safely assert that it will be unnecessary, ma'am. Preston is already amply provided for – he has seen to that. It is partly on this matter that Runner Watts and myself wish to question him.'

Charlotte turned a triumphant look on her aunt.

'What did I say? I knew there was something of the kind behind his urgency to leave us.'

'He seemed anxious to quit the house quickly?'

She nodded. 'Almost before he could obtain an interview with my aunt's lawyer in order to arrange the terms of a pension. I must say it seemed smoky to me.'

He smiled at her. 'Your intuition still works well, Miss Jermyn. Possibly I'll be able to tell you more when I've talked to this man.'

He rose. 'With your permission, Lady Jermyn, perhaps I might be conducted to his quarters? Runner Watts is waiting in the hall and will accompany me.'

She seemed uneasy, but gave the necessary orders to a footman. The servant would have escorted them, but they refused, merely taking directions.

They trod quietly upstairs and reached the valet's room at the back of the house. A knock brought him to the door.

'Mr Trimble, I believe?' asked Justin pleasantly.

CHAPTER XIX

The man facing them changed colour at once. He started to close the door on them, but Watts foiled the intention by deftly inserting a booted foot.

'Open up,' he growled.

The valet obeyed, and they strode into the room, Watts closing the door behind him.

'Now, Mr Trimble,' continued Justin. 'we'd like some account of your – er – dual personality.'

Preston seemed to shrink by inches.

'I don't know what you mean,' he said, in a terrified tone. 'My name's Preston – everyone here knows that – ask the butler – ask my lady – '

'Ah, but what if we were to ask Miss Parker of Madame Yvonne's salon in Bond Street, I wonder?' speculated Justin, in cool tones.

'I – she – ' Preston made a supreme effort to pull himself together. 'I know of no such person,' he protested. 'You're making a mistake, I tell you.'

'Then there seems nothing for it but to confront you with the lady. Tiresome, but if you will have it so – Watts, I suggest we conduct this man to Bow Street for the attention of the magistrate.'

'Very good, sir.'

Watts stepped forward, drawing a pair of handcuffs from his pocket.

'No, no!' cried Preston, starting back. 'I've not committed any crime – not legally, not anything for which I could be arrested – '

'We'll be the judge o' that,' returned Watts. 'But we can't do that unless you speak out, cully!'

Preston swallowed, obviously making a strong effort to control himself and think what best to say.

'Very well, I did give a false name to Miss Parker, but I meant no harm. A man in my station of life needs to have a care,' he said portentously.

'Thinking of committing bigamy, were ye?' asked Watts, with a grin.

'My wife has been dead these ten years or more,' replied Preston, with outraged dignity.

'Then if your intentions towards the lady were honourable,' remarked Justin, 'one doesn't quite see the necessity of sailing under false colours.'

'Because – ' he broke off – 'it's not easy to explain – '

'Might be easier if we mentioned my Lord Pryme's part in the affair,' Watts finished for him.

Preston started. 'You know of that?'

'We knows a deal more than ye thinks for, my cully, but we'd like to hear it from your own mouth. And don't think to fob us off with any gammon, for we've witnesses to testify to the truth.'

'Suppose we sit down?' suggested Justin. 'I believe this may be a lengthy interview.'

'Yes, sir, of course,' answered Preston in a flustered tone, as he set a couple of chairs for them.

'Now,' said Justin, seating himself. 'Begin, if you please, at the point where Pryme first approached you to spy upon your master.'

'It was shortly after the family returned from their visit to Wynsfield, the country house, you know. Lord and Lady St Clare were also staying in the neighbourhood at the same time, and the two families became more closely acquainted. After they returned to London, Lord Pryme began to suspect that Lady St Clare and my master might be meeting in secret – might have become lovers. I don't quite know what his suspicions were founded upon. Except that Ruth, Lady St Clare's maid, is always snooping on her mistress, and I think it likely that he encouraged her to report anything of interest to him.'

'Useful wench, that Ruth,' agreed Watts. She's told us a thing or two about you.'

Fear flickered in Preston's eyes for a moment, diverting him from his recital.

'What kind of things?' he asked, tremulously.

'Never ye mind. Just go on with yer tale. So milord Pryme suspected a liaison between his daughter-in-law and your late master – '

Preston nodded. 'Yes. And the upshot was that he asked me to keep a watch on Sir Aubrey's movements and let him know if I chanced to discover any assignations between the two.'

'I suppose he paid you well for this service?' asked Justin, with a glance of contempt.

'Well, yes.'

'You felt no sense of loyalty towards your master, presumably, even though you had been a trusted servant for over twenty years?'

Preston flushed. 'What sense of loyalty would you feel, sir, towards a man who seduced your daughter and then forced her into leading a life of shame? I'm glad – yes, downright glad! – that he's met his just deserts, damn him!'

'When did all this occur?'

'Nigh on eight months since. My Susan had a respectable situation as second housemaid at Mr Davenport's residence – he's a close friend of Sir Aubrey's. A girl lacking a mother's guidance, and myself too occupied to give her the attention she plainly needed – with a gentleman like Sir Aubrey, what could be expected? In the event, when she lost her situation on account of her condition, and turned to him for help, what did he do but obtain her a position at a gambling hell called Croker's, in Covent Garden – I tell you, the place is a brothel, too! She's there now, to her shame and mine, for try as I will, she won't leave, so I've disowned her for ever! Fortunately she miscarried, so at least I've no grandchild to concern myself over. Perhaps now you'll understand why I was more than willing to fall in with milord Pryme's suggestion?'

Justin nodded. 'Moreover, I would consider you to have a very adequate motive for murder.'

Preston jumped to his feet in alarm.

'I swear to you that I did not murder him! I wanted him punished, true, but why should I swing for him, when he'd done enough harm to me and mine already? I'm not such a fool!'

'Very well. Continue, pray. Where does your courtship of Miss Parker come into this?'

Preston calmed down a little under the influence of Justin's matter of fact tone.

'When I was keeping watch on my master, I noticed him frequently entering the side door at the modiste's premises and remaining somewhere in the building for an hour or more. I reported this to milord Pryme, who questioned Lady St Clare's maid and was told that she, too, paid very frequent visits to the salon, but quite openly in the usual way, with Ruth in attendance. He suspected that in some way they were keeping assignations, so he instructed me to become friendly with one of the staff at the salon with a view to learning more. Miss Parker was the obvious choice – a female entrusted with all the inside workings of the business, and one, moreover, who was a spinster and unlikely to have a follower. There was only one way in which I found it possible to scrape an acquaintance with her, and that was to attend at a Nonconformist chapel where she goes every Sunday. I'm of the Established church myself, but thought this a small price to pay for the end in view.'

'Jesuitical, eh?' murmured Justin.

'I beg your pardon, sir?' Preston seemed puzzled.

'No matter – I meant simply that you felt the end justified the means. But pray continue.'

'It took some time to gain Miss Parker's confidence sufficiently to learn anything to the purpose,' went on Preston, 'but I hit upon the notion of meeting her every so often in the yard of the modiste's shop for just a few minutes in the middle of the day. It was supposed to be to let her know when I could get time off to meet her in the evening, as I could never be sure in advance, when I saw her on Sundays. Of course, I was really hoping that one day she'd take me inside so that I could fathom where Sir Aubrey and the Lady could possibly be meeting. She did at last, one time when the proprietress was absent for a few hours. She took me upstairs from the basement to the passage and rooms leading off it, and hinted at the use to which the private room was sometimes put. Then she showed me the concealed door leading from the salon. That was enough. I reported to my lord, and he told me to be especially watchful of any notes which were delivered by hand to Sir Aubrey. I was unable to get a sight of one for several weeks, though I did once see him burn one. Then came the one delivered to him on Saturday. He left it in the pocket of his dressing gown – as you know, sir – ' turning to Justin – 'for I showed it to you.'

Justin nodded. 'A fact which somewhat puzzles me, I must confess. But you shall explain that hereafter. Pray continue. What did you do next?'

'I took the note to milord, and he identified his daughter-in-law's hand, of course. He was certain that the rendezvous would be at the modiste's after what I had told him, so instructed me to conceal myself near the side street entrance just before two o'clock to see if Sir Aubrey arrived. If so, I was to await Lady St Clare's arrival, then report to milord, who would be loitering about Bond Street in his carriage. Sir Aubrey arrived in a hackney at ten minutes after two, and I heard him tell the jarvey to call for him at four sharp, so then I knew that this was the right place. I began to have doubts, though, when milady took so long in coming – not until a quarter to three.'

'Tell me, what of your arranged meeting with Miss Parker in the yard at ten minutes to two?'

'You know of that, do you, sir?'

'I told ye we've witnesses to a deal of your tale,' put in Watts, 'so ye'd best stick to the truth.'

'I am doing so, Officer,' replied Preston, in a tone of reproof. 'Well, sir, I kept that appointment, but she wasn't there. We never spent more than a few minutes together, so I knew she'd not think it odd if I didn't wait. As a matter of fact, I'd arranged it purposely so that if anyone did see me loitering about the place, they'd take no notice. The staff there were quite used to seeing me meeting Miss Parker.'

'So you reported to Pryme at about three o'clock that the lovebirds were in the nest, and he called at the salon for Lady St Clare at a quarter after three. The excuse was made that she wasn't ready to go, and he called again at five minutes to four. Have you any notion at all as to his whereabouts during that interval?'

A scared look came into Preston's eyes.

'No, sir. I supposed him to be driving round the streets until he thought fit to return for her.'

'He didn't mention his intentions?'

'No, sir.'

'Nor did he let slip what action he proposed to take now that the culprits were caught red-handed?'

Preston shook his head, evidently finding it difficult to speak.

'What did ye think he'd do?' demanded Watts. 'Did ye reckon he'd commit murder?'

'Oh, no, no!' gasped the valet. 'I'm sure I never dreamt of such a thing, else I'd never have had anything to do with the business, little as I liked the man! I'm a law abiding citizen – '

'But ye must have known the Earl'd take some action?'

'I thought perhaps a duel – kept quiet, of course, and on some trumped-up charge, in the way gentlemen do. You can't think –'

'What did *you* do, after you'd reported to Pryme at three o'clock?' Justin put in, suddenly.

Preston started. Evidently his nerve was giving under the strain.

'Why, nothing – that's to say, I returned here to my duties. I laid out Sir Aubrey's evening clothes for the dinner with His Royal Highness.'

'You mean to say you didn't hang about in the vicinity to see what transpired?' asked Justin, incredulously. 'By Jupiter, you must have less curiosity than most men! At what time did you leave? Precisely, please.'

Preston thought for a moment. 'It can't have been any later than twenty minutes after three, sir,' he said at last. 'I waited only to see milord enter the salon. I wished to have nothing more to do with the affair.'

'Washing your hands of it, eh?'

Justin's keen eyes studied the valet for a while, causing him to fidget.

'Hmm. To return to the matter of the note making the

assignation. You found it on Saturday, you told me. Presumably, after showing it to Pryme, you would have returned it to Jermyn's dressing gown pocket in case he went looking for it?'

'That is so, sir.'

'And during the whole of the five days when he was thought to be missing, it didn't occur to you that you could safely destroy it?'

Preston looked uncertain. He shook his head.

'To speak truth, sir, I forgot about it. There were other matters on my mind.'

'Speculations as to where your master might be, perhaps? For of course you had no notion that he was murdered, did you, until Dr Astley Cooper informed Lady Jermyn of that fact?'

The scared look came once more into Preston's face. He shook his head violently.

'It was a lady who protested too much,' said Justin in a meditative voice.

The other two looked puzzled, though Watts gave a faint grin, used to his companion's vagaries.

'Why did you show the note to me, Preston?' Justin asked suddenly, in a different tone. 'Why give me any help at all, since you needed to keep your own part in the affair secret?'

Preston swallowed. 'I – I wanted you to think I was willing to assist you, sir. And I didn't reckon you could learn much from that note, anyway. Perhaps I underestimated you.'

Watts shook his head. 'That's a bad mistake, me old buck. Newgate's full o' felons who've underestimated the law.'

'One more thing,' added Justin, rising to his feet. 'As a valet, you'll be sure to notice a gentleman's attire. Will you tell me precisely what the Earl of Pryme was wearing on the day of Jermyn's murder?'

'So now we know where we are, sir. D'ye reckon he was telling the truth? I've a feeling myself that he was holding something back, though danged if I knew what,' said Watts, in a low tone, as they made their way back to the parlour.

'I'm certain he was. I think he told the truth, more or less, until I asked what he did after reporting to Pryme at three o'clock.'

'Ye don't believe he came back here? Any evidence for that, sir?'

'That given by Sally Bates. She saw a man leaving by the yard gate – almost certainly the murderer, since that was about ten minutes after the shot was fired. Immediately afterwards she heard footsteps going along the passage in the direction of the yard. I postulate that those footsteps were Preston's.'

'Ye think he went in by the street door a second time, after reporting to Lord Pryme?'

Justin nodded. 'I think he may have hung about the premises to see what occurred – much more natural than clearing off at once, as he'd have had us believe. Then he noticed another man entering by the side door and followed him, so witnessing the murder. He may have been in concealment then, but afterwards he'd follow close on the murderer's heels to escape, and the odds are that he knows he was spotted. And that's why he's in too much of a panic at present to tell us. But I'll wager he will before long, if we leave him be, rather than run the risk of falling foul of this villain. Let's hope it won't be too late.'

Watts shook his head gravely; but they could say no more for the present, as they had reached the parlour. Watts took a seat in the hall, while Justin entered the room to rejoin the ladies.

It was not an agreeable surprise to see that in his absence they had received several other morning callers.

CHAPTER XX

Lady Quainton was sitting beside Lady Jermyn on the sofa, while Anthea Rutherford and Charlotte occupied chairs close together. Opposite them sat Lord Escott. He looked more than usually saturnine as his glance rested on Justin.

'Ah, Rutherford,' he said, lazily, half rising from his chair in a perfunctory bow. 'Industrious as ever, I collect. I trust your endeavours will not prove in vain.'

'On the contrary,' returned Justin, turning to greet Cassandra Quainton and his niece. 'I am tolerably satisfied. How do'you do, Godmama? I trust I see you well. And Anthea – what a quiz of a bonnet, dear child – but I dare say it's all the crack.'

Anthea wrinkled her nose at him, putting up her hands to the delectable confection in palest yellow silk which she was wearing.

'Indeed it is – how should you suppose I'd be wearing anything that was not? You may be thankful, my love – ' turning to Charlotte – 'that you don't possess any tiresome bachelor relatives who consider themselves qualified to pass judgment on your attire.'

'Well, I *do* possess a bachelor relative, of course, but I don't feel that we are sufficiently acquainted as yet for him to make any comments of a personal nature,' replied Charlotte, twinkling at Justin. 'But, believe me, I should welcome a little funning now and then. I quite envy you that.'

'Then we must see what we can do to remedy the deficiency,' Justin said, with a challenging look.

'Admirable,' put in Escott, sarcastically. 'He is the most accomplished flirt, is he not, Miss Jermyn? In truth, there's no end to his talents – he quite puts the rest of us into the shade.' He paused for a moment, then added: 'But I really called to see if you would care to drive out with me in the Park, Miss Jermyn, for half an hour or so? That is, if your aunt will permit, of course?'

'Oh, certainly,' said Lady Jermyn, quickly. 'I am quite sure it will do Lottie good – that's to say,' she amended, seeing the reproachful look on her niece's face, 'if she feels equal to it, and wouldn't prefer to sit quietly at home chatting.'

'Perhaps some other time, sir,' put in Charlotte, seeing Escott looking to her for a decision. 'You're very good, but indeed I feel monstrous lazy this morning! Moreover, Anthea has just begun telling me about a ball she attended recently, and I don't need to explain to you the fascination of hearing who was wearing what, I am sure!'

It was said so charmingly that no offence could possibly be taken, even if Escott had not been far too polished to betray any such feelings.

'Naturally I cannot hope to compete with the delights of a discussion on Fashion. It remains with you, my dear Rutherford, to entertain me, I fear. Have you viewed any interesting antiquities lately?'

This produced the intended laugh, and Justin replied in kind. In a few moments, the conversation ceased to be general; the older ladies talked quietly together, the young ones animatedly, while the gentlemen were left to themselves.

'I understand that you've just come from an interview

with Jermyn's valet, Preston,' Escott said, in a low tone. 'May I enquire if he had any information to offer of value in your – ah – investigation?'

'You may, and yes, he had.'

'Indeed? Something which is a certain guide to the perpetrator of the murder?'

Justin shook his head. 'Unfortunately, no. Although I'm persuaded that he is in possession of valuable evidence which he doesn't choose to divulge at present.'

Escott raised his eyebrows. 'You amaze me,' he drawled. 'Why do you suppose he should do that?'

Justin glanced towards the others, but they were still absorbed in their own private conversations.

'Fear – I'd hazard a guess that he feels safe only as long as he keeps mum.'

'Dear me, how very melodramatic. You're quite sure, my dear fellow, that you're not imagining the whole? After all, a long acquaintance with – what is it exactly that you go grubbing around? Ruins, tombs, old bones and objects of that kind must engender an unhealthy, morbid fancy, I fear. I realise that one's valet knows more about one's private life than any other person, but even so I expect you've already learnt all that he can tell you.'

'Did you know that he was spying on Jermyn?' Justin asked suddenly.

Escott gave a cynical smile. 'I had observed as much from his behaviour. For Pryme, I think. So you've discovered that! I congratulate you. It should certainly offer you some guidance.'

'Perhaps. One thing I'm curious about, and that is your reticence about the connection between Jermyn and Madame Yvonne, when I first asked for your help in this affair. I've since discovered that you could have told me the whole, instead of merely hinting at it, had you chosen to do so.'

'The devil you have! Well – ' with one of his unpleasant smiles – 'I must confess that I rather enjoyed throwing out a tit bit of information that I considered fairly useless. You received it so eagerly, like a cur with a bone.'

'Doubtless you're familiar with the habits of curs. I should thank you, even so, as it turned out to be far from useless.'

'I think, you know, Rutherford, that one could be in danger of underestimating you,' Escott said, as he rose to take his leave. 'Your little games are perhaps not so harmless as they appear.'

After Justin Rutherford and the Bow Street Runner left him, Preston collapsed in a chair, giving way to the uneasy feelings that beset him. He had been a fool not to admit to everything at once – or had he? Was there anything to be gained in keeping quiet about what he knew? Dangerous knowledge; the best course for him was to clear out and bury himself in the depths of the country somewhere. He had the money for that, now.

There would be no pension from Lady Jermyn, though. Damn that interfering man Rutherford, who had told her of the arrangement between himself and Pryme; and damn even more thoroughly Lady St Clare's busybody of a maid, Ruth, who had supplied the detectives with that information. Could he possibly screw some more money out of the murderer? He shivered. Too risky by half. Best leave matters as they stood; otherwise he might find himself the next victim.

He was too vulnerable here, in the Jermyn residence, that was certain. Why should he not clear out today, while he was still safe? He would go along to the coach station straight away, book a ticket for – where? Somewhere in Sussex, he thought, because he was not unfamiliar with the country, having been with Sir Aubrey at Wynsfield throughout the years. Then he would come back, pack up his belongings, and take a hackney to the coach station. Simple enough, he thought.

He used the servants' staircase which led past the kitchens. Cook came out as he was walking along the passage, and gave him a friendly nod.

'Going out for a bit, Mr Preston? Don't blame ye – there's naught to keep ye in nowadays, be there?' She heaved a heartfelt sigh that shook her not inconsiderable bulk. 'Dearie me, it's sad doings, that it be, and no mistake! I never had the like in all my years in service, I can tell ye!'

He agreed briefly, and hurried on his way to the door leading to the area steps.

He was about to run up them to the gate which gave on to the street, when he heard the front door at the main entrance closing behind a visitor.

He froze where he stood.

A man descended the front steps to the street. Peering up from the well of the area, Preston was able to identify Escott.

He hung back, waiting until Escott had merged into the other passers-by before venturing into the street himself. The fewer people who saw him now until he was safe in his chosen haven, the better.

It was fortunate that he did not know he was being kept under surveillance by a person of no less experience than Runner Joseph Watts. A word in the Runner's ear as Justin had turned to enter Lady Jermyn's parlour after their interview with Preston, had made provision for this.

When he reached the coach office, a disappointment awaited him. All the coaches leaving for Sussex that day were already fully booked; he would be obliged to delay his departure until tomorrow. There was nothing to be done, since although he was in possession of a large sum of money, he was not minded to squander any of it in posting charges. He therefore booked a ticket for Brighton and, swallowing his chagrin as best he might, took an economical return to Curzon Street on foot.

The Earl of Pryme was at home, the butler announced graciously, and would be pleased to see my Lord Escott, if his lordship would have the goodness to follow him to the bookroom.

The pleasure was obviously an overstatement, Escott reflected cynically, as he studied Pryme's lowering countenance with amusement.

'Don't often see you here, Escott,' his host greeted him. 'Sit down, won't you? Will you take anything?'

'A glass of madeira might not come amiss, I thank you,' returned Escott, seating himself in a wing chair opposite Pryme. 'Not that I'd wish to put you to any trouble,' he added, with a sneer.

'You wouldn't,' returned Pryme, ungraciously.

Nevertheless, he rang the bell, and a footman appeared to dispense the refreshment.

'Your very good health,' said Escott insincerely, as he raised his glass. 'That's to say, one really does trust it will remain so, my dear fellow.'

Pryme set down his glass sharply.

'And pray what does that mean?'

'Families are the very devil, are they not'? asked Escott, in a vague tone. 'Especially perhaps beautiful and charming daughters – or daughers-in-law, of course. No saying what starts they may be getting up to, is there?'

Pryme's face reddened, 'Just what d'ye mean?'

'Probably nothing. On the other hand, one can't be certain. Perhaps I should explain. I've just come, you see, from Lady Jermyn's.'

'Well?'

'I saw there, besides the lady and her delightful niece, that tiresome, but I'm afraid I must say successful – ah – investigator – Justin Rutherford.'

Pryme snorted. 'Interferin' busybody! What's a feller of his class want with snoopin' around in matters that don't concern him? What are the Bow Street Runners for?'

'Precisely what I asked him, but, you know, he's quite unrepentant. And he does seem to have made some headway in solving the late unfortunate Jermyn's murder.'

Pryme gave him a keen look. 'Does he indeed?'

'Yes. He was there not only to flirt with Miss Jermyn – ' Escott's teeth bared in a savage smile – 'which he does very adroitly, one must confess, but also to interrogate Preston, Jermyn's valet.'

Pryme's hand jerked suddenly, spilling his wine. He swore, mopping at his jacket with a handkerchief.

'The devil he was! D'ye know what was said? I mean, have you any notion if – '

'I know exactly what you mean,' sneered Escott. 'And I can say with certainty that he is well informed as to Preston's activities under an alias.'

Pryme made a choking sound.

'Damn that fellow to hell, I paid him blood money to keep his trap shut! Does he – has he – do you know if he's told everything?'

'Everything?'

Escott raised his eyebrows, and for a moment the two men stared at each other in silence. Then Escott shook his head.

'Rutherford is of the opinion that Preston has yet more to reveal, but fear keeps him silent.' He paused. 'How long that silence will last depends, I surmise, upon two factors. One is, how long it takes him to realise that keeping his knowledge to himself is dangerous. The other – '

'That someone else may decide to prolong it,' finished Pryme, grimly.

'I see we understand each other. Permit me to explain a plan which came to mind.'

Preston read the note over for the third or fourth time. It had been delivered by hand, and stated simply that Sir George Jermyn would like to see Preston on a matter of business that would be to his advantage. Not having any fixed residence in Town as yet, Sir George suggested that Preston should wait on him at Croker's Club in King Street. The porter would direct him to a private room. Sir George would expect him at half past eight this evening.

Just like the Quality, thought Preston resentfully, always taking it for granted that you would do as they say. Croker's Club! He had no wish to go there, where he might meet with that shameless hussy, his daughter. On the other hand, a private room – no need to see her at all. Besides, something to his advantage. Would that be the offer of a situation with the new baronet at Wynsfield?

He reflected. He might do worse, for a few years at any rate. If he kept quiet, lay low there in Sussex, things would blow over. It would be seen that he had no intention of peaching on anybody. He would be safe.

He glanced at the clock on his mantelshelf. Time for dinner in the servants' hall. There would be a long enough interval afterwards for him to make up his mind whether or not he would keep this appointment. He replaced the note on a small table that served him as a writing desk.

It was there that Watts, slipping in unobserved by the garden door while the staff were at table and making his way to Preston's room, found it and noted its contents.

Croker's Club in King Street appeared no different outside from the buildings surrounding it, a discreet Town house approached by a short flight of steps flanked by wrought iron railings. Inside, however, the foyer was ablaze with light from a handsome crystal chandelier, and deep red carpet muffled the footsteps.

A liveried porter approached to greet Preston civilly enough; but his eyes flickered towards two large individuals who were hovering nearby.

'Good evening. I am expected by Sir George Jermyn,' said Preston, with more assurance than he felt.

The porter gave an infinitesimal motion of his head towards the bulky attendants, who withdrew to a discreet distance.

'Of course. I will find someone to conduct you to the private room.'

Another gesture brought a flunkey to whom the porter gave his instructions. Eyeing Preston contemptuously, the man conducted him up an elegant twisting staircase to a passage at the top. A few yards along this, he opened a door on the right which led into a small room, evidently an antchamber, for Preston was conducted through yet another door into a larger room.

'Be pleased to wait here,' the servant instructed him, and pointed to a chair.

He then withdrew, closing the door behind him.

Preston sat down uneasily on the edge of the chair.

Time passed, and his uneasiness increased. He pulled out his watch, and saw that it was turned a quarter to nine. He had come early, of course, so that made the waiting seem longer. It was nothing for the Quality to be quarter of an hour late. Nevertheless, he fidgeted.

He was in a state of high tension when suddenly a door which he had not observed before was pushed open, and a man entered the room.

Preston started to his feet. This was not the man he had

expected. This was the last person he wished to see.

'Mr Preston. Sit down again. You may as well, for you and I are going to have a little talk.'

The other seated himself and nodded encouragingly.

'But – but – Sir George Jermyn – I came here to meet him – '

'A ruse, I'm sorry to say. I fear you would not have come to see me, would you? But I observe from your expression that you would not. Don't worry – I shan't detain you long.'

The assurance did nothing to calm Preston's panic. He clenched his hands until the nails bit into the flesh.

'Cast your mind back to the afternoon of your late master's sad demise. You'd been spying upon him, as ordered. You followed him into the modiste's side door, saw him with the lady, and returned to the street to report. That is correct?'

Preston nodded wordlessly.

'So far, so good. And then you loitered about for a while before entering that door a *second time* in pursuit of someone else.'

Preston sprang to his feet again, shaking.

'No – no!'

'Oh, but yes, my friend. You followed this individual after a prudent interval, concealing yourself – now, where would it be?'

He looked at the terrified valet for inspiration, but gained no response other than a choking sound.

'Probably on the staircase. It was only a temporary expedient; for after looking through the spyhole in the workroom and ascertaining that the lady had fled and Jermyn was alone, the intruder left that room and entered the next. That would be when you came down from the staircase and took a look through the spyhole for yourself. And what, pray, did you see?'

Preston flung up his hands in a defensive gesture.

'Nothing!' he stammered. 'Nothing! I didn't see you shoot Sir Aubrey – I mean – I – I – oh, God! I wasn't there, I wasn't, I tell you!'

The last words were shouted in hysteria.

'Thank you.' The calm tones were in sinister contrast to Preston's agitation. 'I knew that must have been the way of it, when I chanced to espy you behind me as I made my escape along the lane leading from the mews. A pity I turned round, don't you think? For now you must go, too, my friend.'

He rose and produced a pistol from his pocket.

A flying form erupted through the door at his back seizing the pistol before he could use it.

'None o' that,' said Watts sternly, passing the weapon over to Justin who had followed close on his heels. 'I'm arresting ye, Lord Escott, for the murder of Sir Aubrey Jermyn. We heard every word ye said to this man here, so there's no use in denying it. Best come quietly.'

He reached a pair of handcuffs from his pocket.

'One moment before you manacle me,' said Escott. 'I'll come freely, but first I beg the favour of a few words with Mr Rutherford.'

Watts cocked an eyebrow at Justin.

'What d'you say to that, sir?'

'Let be for the moment. Take Preston away and wait outside.'

'Reckon he can't try any tricks,' said Watts, glancing at the pistol in Justin's hand. 'Ye've only to call, guv'nor, all the same.'

When the door had closed behind the others, the two men faced each other challengingly.

'I wouldn't have done it, y'know,' said Escott, in his usual drawling tone, 'if it hadn't been for our final disagreement. I'd disliked the fellow for long enough – I think you know all the reasons. But I needed all the income from this place – only for a time, say six months, to enable me to meet recent unfortunate reverses. Matters would have righted themselves after that. He wouldn't agree. We argued the point back and forth on that fateful Monday morning, but nothing would persuade him.' He shrugged. 'After that, naturally, there was only one course open to me. I knew he was to keep an assignation at Yvonne's with Stella St Clare. I was familiar with the usual procedure. It seemed a highly suitable place for terminating the existence of one who had always been a thorn in my flesh.'

Justin nodded. 'So that was it. Have you anything more to say before I hand you over to the law?'

He was holding the pistol negligently in his hand by this time.

Escott suddenly seized it from him. Then, as Justin moved to grapple with him, Escott placed it to his own head, and fired.

'Devilish complicated,' commented Edward Rutherford.

Justin had just finished explaining the sequence of events leading to the solution of the mystery.

'Indeed it was. First we had a vanishing husband, then a corpse in unexpected surroundings. Once we found out that the murder actually took place at the modiste's shop, we could then build a structure on which to work towards a solution. We were bedevilled by motives, though.'

'Don't surprise me. Demmed loose fish, Jermyn; even if one shouldn't speak ill of the dead.'

'No lack of suspects who might have had the opportunity, but no concrete proof until the girl Sally Bates told Watts of the man she'd seen slipping out of the back way just at the crucial time. She described what he was wearing, too, which was a vital link. When I asked Preston to describe Pryme's attire on that same afternoon, the account was completely different. I was able to check that with Madame Yvonne, and then I knew Escott must be our man.'

'Puzzles me how you first tumbled to that valet chap's activities. Later, of course, when you heard he'd been blackmailing Pryme – but you seem to have had your eye on him before that.'

'Yes, I believe I did. I found it odd, you see, right from the first interview with him, that he spoke of Jermyn in the *past* tense. Yet he was supposed not to know where his employer was. Then there was the follower who appeared for poor Miss Parker out of nowhere, to vanish later just as suddenly. The report of the blackmailing clinched it for me, of course. I must admit, Ned, that I deliberately set Preston up as a decoy duck when I was talking to Escott after our final interview with the valet. We needed to force Escott out into the open, and Preston was safe enough with Watts keeping surveillance on him. Good thing Escott shot himself – less scandal for the Jermyns.'

Edward nodded. 'It's an unpleasant business for them altogether, but fortunately memories are short in Town. Some fresh *on dit* next week, I dare say. Shall we join the ladies?'

Justin followed him into the drawing room and took a seat beside Charlotte, who with her aunt had been dining at the Rutherfords' house that evening.

'I wish to thank you, Mr Rutherford,' she said, with one of her enchanting smiles. 'I think my aunt has already tried to do so, but you wouldn't allow her to say a word. You shan't fob me off so easily – we truly are vastly in your debt.'

He laughed. 'Say no more, ma'am, or I may feel obliged to present you with a reckoning.'

Her eyes twinkled, but she felt herself blushing. She thought it time to change the subject.

'We are to take a month's holiday at East Bourne in a day or two. Mr Leasowe has found us a most desirable lodging, and we're both looking forward to a change of air.'

'I sincerely trust you will benefit. I'm going out of Town myself shortly, though I'm not yet sure where. Greece – Turkey – or the north of England – '

'You're an incurable wanderer, sir.'

'So I am. But I think our paths may cross again.'